DIDIER DAENINCKX, France's leading crime novelist, has written more than forty books. His novel *Murder in Memoriam* forced the French government to try Nazi collaborators, convicted the collaborator Paul Touvier to life imprisonment, and led President François Mitterrand to declare July 16 a day of national reflection on fascism and racism in France. He is also the author of *A Very Profitable War*. Also a journalist and an author of literary fiction, he won the 2012 Prix Goncourt for his book *L'espoir en contrabande*.

ANNA MOSCHOVAKIS is the translator of Albert Cossery's *The Jokers* and Georges Simenon's *The Engagement*, among other books. She is also a poet and an editor at Ugly Duckling Presse.

NAZIS IN THE METRO

DIDIER DAENINCKX

TRANSLATED BY ANNA MOSCHOVAKIS

MELVILLE HOUSE
BROOKLYN · LONDON

MELVILLE
INTERNATIONAL
CRIME

MELVILLE INTERNATIONAL CRIME

NAZIS IN THE METRO

First published in France as *Nazis dans le métro* in 1997
Copyright © 1997 by Éditions Baleine, Paris, France
Published by arrangement with Mon Agent et Compagnie
6 rue de Victor Hugo—73000, Chambéry, France
Translation copyright © 2014 by Anna Moschovakis

First Melville House Printing: March 2014

Melville House Publishing   8 Blackstock Mews
    145 Plymouth Street   and   Islington
    Brooklyn, NY 11201   London N4 2BT

mhpbooks.com   facebook.com/mhpbooks   @melvillehouse

Library of Congress Control Number: 2014933228

ISBN: 978-1-61219-296-3

Manufactured in the United States of America
1 3 5 7 9 10 8 6 4 2

NAZIS IN THE METRO

1

JAURÈS AND FUNÈS

Sloga had read the *Indépendant de Perpignan* while down-ing an uninspiring coffee on the terrace of the Trois Grâces café, just before hitting the road. Murdered children, ethnic cleansing, a prince's divorce, the usual filth. The only touch of humanity was in the almanac, next to the weather report: an item recalling the assassination of Jean Jaurès, eighty-one years earlier to the day, the 31st of July, 1914. He had not known that this disappearance was compensated for, a few hours later, by the birth of the comedian Louis de Funès. A conscience, pawned for its weight in funny faces: the cen-tury was off on the right track.

The Autoroute des Deux Mers snaked and dipped. Un-dulations in the land concealed the Catharist past the vil-lages were now selling off, stone by stone: their erstwhile resistance embellished labels on bottles of Corbières; their sacrificed villages attracted euro-wielding tourists; their marginalized faith inspired spectacles of Sound and Light. He didn't blame them; the entire country, a republic of au-tophagics, was living on its own remains. In the last few days, the waves of suntanned Spaniards and Italians had slowly begun to drift northward, and he was surprised not to be making any progress toward Roquemaure. When he recognized the sound of ambulances chirping in the distance, he understood that the traffic jam was actually a spontaneous funeral procession. The people who now lay dead in crumpled metal heaps where the Languedoc Route met the Autoroute du Soleil couldn't have dreamed of drawing such a crowd to their services. Sloga slowly advanced alongside the red-and-white clown hats that surrounded the accident scene and first-aid zone, trying not to look at the disemboweled suitcases, the metallic shimmer of emergency blankets, the bottles turned upside down over IV tubes.

For some ten kilometers, his foot was lighter on the gas, and then, gradually, it began to recover its sense of weight. He enjoyed long, solitary trips. Driving calmed him down, and, as he no longer dreamed, it gave his mind the opportunity to wander in total freedom. He would talk to himself, sing, arrange sounds according to nothing but the obscure meaning of their rhythm. The place names marked with arrows on the brown signs that lined the road were so many memory traps. Every now and then, a memory gave rise to a burst of nostalgia, and he let the ghosts rush in until their features were reflected clearly in the windshield, floating above the shifting landscape. Then he would concentrate on the three-pointed star stuck to the tip of the hood and breathe deeply, to disengage with anything beyond the tangible world. Protesting grape growers had taken over the tollbooths at Ury. They would let you through for the price of a smile.

He tossed the yellow tract onto the passenger seat and read it at an angle as he descended into Paris. He entered the capital via a tentacle of the ring road and drove along its cultivated banks. There was almost nothing left of the neighborhood where he'd roamed as a child. Not even the name. The glory of Bercy's wine-trading past was no longer the first thing that came to most people's minds. At best, they might think of the Palais Omnisports, but more likely it would be the omnipresent Minister of Finance. Dust from construction sites dulled the sparkle on the tiles of the old pneumatic factory, a bulldozer's claws attacked the cement rotunda near the refrigeration warehouses, and a perforated metal barrier blocked off Rue Watt. What was left of a world that had been built by labor was being erased so that the book stacks for the grand library could be erected in its place: four massive, glassed-in legs of a gigantic table turned on its head. Wherever you looked, placards announced ambitious building projects along the Seine, and he wondered once again if the Opéra Bastille, the Abattoir des Sciences et Techniques, and the Arche de la Défense were built in response to real needs, or if their construction was not, rather, a pretext for reclaiming whole segments of working-class Paris.

He crossed over the Austerlitz tracks on the Tolbiac bridge, which a municipal architect had repainted red, white, and green like a pizzeria, and activated the remote-controlled door to the parking garage as soon as the building on the corner of Rue Jeanne d'Arc came into view. The nose of the Mercedes tilted toward the basement, where the fluorescent lights flickered on and off until their autopsy glow settled on the cars squeezed tightly between rough pillars. He parked between two Clios near the elevator door on Level 2, and gathered up the objects that had scattered around the car's interior over the course of his trip. It wasn't until he was making his way around to the trunk to retrieve his luggage that he became aware of a presence. Nothing concrete, not the movement of a shadow, nor the sound of breathing, nor the squeaking of soles, only the weight of someone's eyes, someone's attention.

He froze, his hand on the car, and turned around to take a long look at the garage. He blinked. The tens of thousands of painted white dashes on the roadway between Narbonne and Paris had left their imprint on his retinas. He shook his head to dispel their traces as much as his own uneasiness. He had to use both hands to pick up the suitcase, which was weighed down by books. The lights went out just as he stopped in front of the elevator. The call button was not illuminated as usual. He felt around for it, then pressed it several times, tugging the door toward himself out of instinct. It opened. A man was huddled on the floor of the elevator car, his silhouette reflected in its mirrored back wall. Sloga backed up and into another man, who had snuck up silently behind him under the cover of darkness. He blurted out a ridiculous "Pardon me" before the first punches fell.

2

BRÉTONNADES

Gabriel Lecouvreur, also known as the Octopus, extracted himself from the compact Peugeot like a crab from a shoebox. The periwinkle-clad meter maids hadn't yet started scouring for miscreants on this side of the Place Léon Blum, and he figured he had time to go have his coffee before the windshield of Cheryl's car was graced with a city-issued ticket. The news seller, inside the illuminated, ad-covered walls of his tiny kiosk, was tying up yesterday's unsold papers. He had arrayed the day's wares in misshapen, unstable waves on the counter. Gabriel managed to withdraw a *Parisien* and a *Libération* more or less intact, without endangering the precarious equilibrium. Not long ago, just the sight of someone flipping through the first of these lying rags would have constituted an act of war. But now, surprisingly, he found himself more interested and engaged by its provincial reportage than by the sententious editorials in his other standby for daily news. And yet, he was sure he hadn't changed ...

A commercial moving truck pulled up in front of the wooden table-leg manufacturer's place on Rue Godefroy-Cavaignac. A team of burly, taciturn men began loading machine parts, strapping them in place somewhere in the dark belly of the semi. Gabriel approached Monsieur Alaric the elder, proprietor of the table-leg operation, a portly Breton with olive skin who was watching the movers' comings and goings through a double door. He extended his hand. The pressure of his fingers was more than just weak: it was disillusioned.

—No rest for the weary, eh! What are you doing, modernizing? Getting rid of the old rigs?

The carpenter shrugged.

—Modernize? What for? With table legs, it's not like you're cutting them with lasers and scouring the Internet every morning to find out if some cabinetmaker in Fatchakulla has invented a revolutionary new technique in the middle of the night!

—So what are they doing then?

Alaric unzipped the front pocket of his overalls and dug out a Gauloise Light from a dented packet.

—Isn't it obvious? I'm out of here.

He offered Gabriel a cigarette.

—Thanks, but I haven't quit quitting … You're really leaving? Closing up shop? Is business that bad?

Smoke streamed from his nostrils in two jets that merged into one.

—You kidding? I've got a list of orders as long as a day without bread … No, the new owner's kicking me out. There's no romance in table legs anymore. He wants to gut the place and turn it into a gallery-café …

—Another café! Well, we don't have to worry about dying of hunger in this neighborhood anymore … And where will you go? Back to Brittany?

Alaric nearly choked.

—Brittany, me? Never! I don't even go there for vacation! I need streets, bars, cars, subways! The older generations might've had a hard time adapting, but I'm completely at home ...

Gabriel leaned his long frame against the wall.

—Of course, it's been a long time ... The Alaric name has been on this shack forever ...

—You can say that again! Now we're out on the street ... It was my great-grandfather who came here first, from Finistère-Nord, at the end of the last century ... The recruiters arrived and sent whole villages into exile, giving advances to parents and wives ... Reimbursable from the first year's pay. It was a little like Citroën and Bouygues with the Moroccans and the Turks ... But with us it was for the first Delaunay Belleville cars. The plant was in Saint-Denis, not far from Briche. Steel frames, spoked wheels, wood interiors, all-leather upholstery ... They needed the best craftsmen in the country, and they went looking for them in Brittany and Auvergne ... I never had the chance to know my great-grandfather, but my grandfather lived basically the same shitty life as he did ... At first he didn't speak a word of French, and on Saturday nights, after their shifts, Parisian workers would unwind by chasing down "foreigners" ... Because they spoke Méteque, because they were unmarried, because they didn't eat the food everyone else ate. He was systematically beat up ... And you know what the bastards called those raids?

—No.

With an expert flick, Alaric propelled his cigarette butt into the clear waters of the gutter.

—*Brétonnades!* Can you imagine? Forty years before the *ratonnades** against the Arabs ... It's only proof that nothing ever changes: we just get used to it ...

—And where will you go?

—When they ruin the provinces for you and then kick you out of the city, what's left?

Gabriel Lecouvreur's eyebrows rearranged themselves into a circumflex.

—I don't know ...

—It's obvious: the outskirts ... They're sticking me with three thousand square meters in Montreuil, along the highway. It's called Mosinor ... Twelve stories surrounded by a truck route. Three-quarters of the building is occupied by sweatshops, and the courtyard is used as a parking lot for those green dumpsters from the Department of Household Waste! It's a dream come true!

—You do make it sound appealing ... You should reinvent yourself as a real-estate agent. Is there anywhere to get a drink, at least?

—Oh sure, these are civilized people, after all: they just opened a Burger King on the ground floor ... I'm going to have to get used to soft drinks ...

---

* The term *ratonnade*, deriving from "raton" (rat), a racial slur, referred originally to acts of violence in France against people of North African descent during the years of the French-Algerian war (1954–1962). By extension, the term has been used since then to refer to other racially motivated acts of violence.

Gabriel Lecouvreur walked back up toward Ledru-Rollin, his *Parisian* open against the crowd, his nose deep in the news of the rotating orb beneath his feet. The other pedestrians made way for this beanpole of a man absorbed in the world's progress. Some lifted their heads in his direction, and the oldest among them saw in him a strong resemblance to a young Philippe Clay.

Perched on a wobbly stool, on tiptoes, Maria was writing the list of appetizers and desserts of the day on the front window of the Pied de Porc à la Sainte-Scolasse. Lecouvreur stopped next to her. Thanks to the stool, their heads were at the same height. He gave her a kiss on the cheek and pointed at the menu.

—Vinaigrette is written with a V, not a W …

She spun around reflexively to check her writing, realizing as she turned that he was teasing her. She responded in an exaggerated Teruel accent:

—I don't understand … it weally is leeks wit' winaigwette …

The proprietor, who was busy fiddling with the coffee machine, didn't see him enter. Gabriel greeted the fifteen or so regulars gathered around the counter and sat down behind the row of potted Wandering Jews whose leaves, which Maria doped up with aspirin and a concoction of ground eggshells, were as green as the hills of Normandy. Léon, the epileptic German Shepherd, headed toward him in slow motion, his hindquarters skidding. He plowed his muzzle twice into the plastic lattice-backed chairs before collapsing with a sigh at Gabriel's feet. Gérard, who had just finished serving a dozen coffees and almost as many glasses of Calvados, walked across the room. He set down Gabriel's daily bowl of Arabica and a croissant.

—No more sweets for Léon, he's becoming blind as a bat! It's bad enough that he can't bark anymore ...

Ordinarily, Gabriel would have bestowed a thousand virtues on the dog's gluttony; he would have patiently explained that, in *The Symposium*, Plato had the Philosopher assert the palate's superiority over sight, arguing that our eyes detect only the surface of things whereas our taste buds are able to decipher the secret depths of all the flavors of the earth. In other words, he would have put on his usual show. The customers waited attentively for the joust to begin, but it did not; Gabriel remained immobile, waylaid by the News in Brief. Gérard tried again to spark an exchange with a noisy sniff.

—You don't think he stinks?

This attempt met with no greater success. He was preparing to resume his position behind the bar when Gabriel raised his head with a devastated look in his eyes.

—Have you read this?

Gérard leaned over the minuscule box of text to which the Octopus was pointing, at the foot of the page:

ATTACKED IN THE BASEMENT

A man was found gravely wounded in the underground parking lot at 2 Rue Jeanne d'Arc (in the 13th Arrondissement). Robbery was the apparent motive of the attack. The victim, a resident of the

building, 78-year-old André Sloga, was taken to
the Pitié-Salpêtrière hospital, where he remains in
a deep coma.

The proprietor shrugged.

—That's what put you in such a state? There's no respect
anymore, especially for old people. Those stories are a dime
a dozen around here! ...

Gabriel placed his finger on the victim's name.

—Sloga ... André Sloga, the name means nothing to
you?

—Why, should it?

—Actually, yes ... You haven't read *The Innocents, Hell's
Harvest*, even *Weekend in Nagasaki*?

Maria, whose breasts were exactly level with the counter,
had begun to take orders. Gérard admitted his ignorance.

—I've never heard of him ... Who is he, a writer?

—Yes, and not just any writer ... He was a working-
class kid from the south of Paris ... His father worked like
a slave in an alloy plant in Vitry and on Sundays played
accordion at the dance clubs on the banks of the Marne.
Anarcho-pacifist, bit of a basher, borderline alcoholic ... He
writes about it in his first book ...

—Now that you mention it, I'm beginning to place
him ... Weren't they also athletes?

—Not exactly, but almost. In '37, around the time of
Guernica, the father and son got involved in the International Brigades. They were assigned to the defense of the
People's Olympiad in Barcelona, a competition that was
to have taken place at the same time as the Nazi Games in

Berlin, at the opening of which, we all too often forget, our beloved sportsmen, with images of Baron de Coubertin* in their minds, coughed up a raised-arm salute to the Führer! Sloga recounts all of this in detail in *The Innocents*, which Gallimard published in June of 1940, causing a full-scale debacle ... Almost the entire edition was pulped after the superior race cleansed the reading committee—

Maria interrupted him.

—I've only been acquainted with your Sloga for five minutes, but I have a feeling he hasn't had a lot of luck in his life ...

Gabriel tore a crusty point from his croissant and dunked it into his steaming coffee.

—Well, the book ends with the death of his father, who was executed by supporters of Franco ... It's there in everything he writes, every word, story, every tangent, and at the heart of it all: pulsating, bleeding life ... Basically, everything that's missing from almost all the others.

Gérard leapt over to the coffee machine to loosen the handle of a portafilter Maria was wrestling with.

—It's strange that you've never spoken of him before ... We've fought over Calet, Hardellet, André Laude, de Bove, but this guy: nothing. He's fallen through the cracks ... How do you explain that?

Gabriel leaned over his bowl, his hands gripping its porcelain sides, and, lips protruding like a giraffe's, inhaled in one go more than half of the liquid inside.

* Pierre de Coubertin was the French founder of the International Olympic Committee.

—The hard times never left him. After the War, Gallimard published a half-dozen titles by Sloga, until one day they turned one down … He'd written too pointedly about the free use of the guillotine in Algerian prisons, and the Gestapo-style torture the French army was endorsing in the Aurès mountains … This was in 1955. He left Gallimard and slammed the door on his way out … Twenty years later his fury would have made him famous; his fatal flaw was that he was ahead of his time … After that, he floated from publisher to publisher … The last thing of his I read was *Countercurrent* from Plasma in the middle of the 1980s. To my knowledge, he hasn't published anything for more than ten years … Total oblivion. The guy who cranked out that article today didn't even know who he was writing about …

—Give him a call so he can print a correct …

—I have better things to do in life than to call out journalists!

3

THE BLACK LION'S MUSTACHE

Gabriel Lecouvreur got to his car at the precise moment when the traffic warden for Place Léon Blum was tearing the ticket from its stub. She ignored the hand he held out to her, and, without a glance at her victim, tucked the slip of paper under the left wiper blade as procedure required. During the vacation month of August, the streets were beset by repairs that necessitated endless detours, allowing statisticians to observe that summer car travel by Parisians was trending toward the annual norm. He crossed the Seine on the Austerlitz bridge and parked in the shade of the tracks of the elevated metro. One of two white-shirted men in the sentry booth cast him an indifferent glance as he crossed the median.

Six months earlier, when Gabriel had been investigating abusive psychiatric internments, the president of a human-rights organization—who had himself suffered the rigors of a prolonged sojourn between padded walls—dragged him to every hospital in Paris and its vicinity to show him the secret equipment used by state-employed psychiatrists. This self-proclaimed President of the Falsely Diagnosed harbored a pronounced taste for the clandestine. When they'd visited the Pitié-Salpêtrière, he'd asked to meet Gabriel in an infamous parking lot at Port Austerlitz. Gabriel had to knock four times—long, long, short, short—on the side of the electrician's van that served as the man's cover, and await verification before the door slid open. He folded himself in two to enter the vehicle. The president traded his mechanic's overalls for jeans and a sweater. He asked the Octopus to wait, then crouched before a mirror hanging from a strap to fit a jet-black wig on his bald head. After the approximate application of a mustache to match the hair, using his right index finger and a tin of Black Lion shoe polish, the character transformation was complete. From his booth, the sentry of the Salpêtrière had been watching them approach from far away. The mocking smile on his lips blossomed into outright mirth when, as the men passed through the gate, one of the gusts of wind typical to the area caused the president's rug to rotate a quarter-turn. His attempt to re-position his synthetic mane led only to disaster: the sleeve of his pullover, which was too big for him, brushed against his nose and jaw, marring the face of the Defender of Lunatics with black streaks. Gabriel was about to turn back, but his guide, not realizing that his wig was on backwards and his mustache had procreated, shot him an encouraging wink to signify that he had the situation under control.

Vaguely ashamed, Gabriel Lecouvreur now lowered his head while passing the sentry booth for the second time in his existence. He made a beeline for the main entrance while one of the guards was busy answering the phone. He admired the shapeliness of a West Indian woman who was updating a schedule that hung on the wall, lingering for a while on the curve of her waist, then decided to cough to attract her attention.

—Can you tell me which unit André Sloga is in? He's a relative … He was admitted during the night, after an attack …

Her lacquered nails squeaked against the glossy paper of the patient log, and the sharp point of her index finger stopped next to a name.

—He's still in Emergency, in ICU … I'm sorry, but visitors are strictly forbidden.

Gabriel made as if to leave, then turned back around.

—I came up from the south just to see him. Maybe I can find out something from the doc … Do you know who's on his case?

The young woman shrugged, then glanced back at the register.

— Professor Lehmann is taking care of him. You're welcome to try, but I'd be shocked if he agreed to tell you anything whatsoever!

Gabriel was again turned away when he approached the ICU staff to ask for news about Sloga's condition. He waited for a while, pacing the hundred feet of the central corridor, peering at anyone who came or went, his eyes peeled for a crack in the system. Finally he'd had enough, and then, as he was traversing the wings of the Pitié on his way to the exit, he came across a nurse busily picking up books that had fallen from a cart whose shelves, intended for trays of food, had been stocked with reading material instead. He stooped to glean a few copies of *Que sais-je?*—a booklet for the Assimil method of learning English—and two mismatched volumes of *Jalna*, and offered them to the young woman.

—I wasn't aware that hospitals had added reading to their list of treatments ...

She rose and tugged at the bottom of her smock to cover her knees.

—There are lots of sick people who can't stand television anymore, who find it mind-numbing, and ask for things to read instead. I'm in charge of the library ...

Gabriel collected the last paperbacks scattered in the corridor. Then he, too, stood up.

—It's curious ...

After a weighty silence, she took the bait.

—What's curious?

—Oh! Nothing ... I just learned that there's a writer on the verge of death, two steps from here ... And to see all these books on the ground ... It's just strange, the coincidence ...

The librarian's face lit up.

—You mean André Sloga? Do you know André Sloga?

—Not personally; I know him through his writing ... Just yesterday I was rereading *The Innocents* ... A masterpiece. I would very much like to have met him, but your colleagues aren't letting anyone near him.

She pushed her cart over to a small circular room set up as a cafeteria and sat down on a chair.

—There's no point, you would only see a swollen face with tubes in its nose and mouth ... I've read all of his books, passionately; it's unbearable to see someone who has moved you so much in a condition like that ... I was a nurse before I was a librarian, and believe me, I'm used to worse sights ... But with this, it was like the first time ...

—He's badly banged up?

She swayed her head back and forth, lost in her thoughts.

—Yes ... he's a mess. You wonder how he managed to survive ...

This was the trademark of professional thugs, Gabriel thought, the final stroke of intimidation: to leave the target on the verge of death, one foot in, one foot out.

—Do they know what happened?

—Not really ... From what I've been told, one of his neighbors discovered him slumped in the stairway to the parking lot in his building, around one in the morning. Some cops from Boulevard de l'Hôpital brought him to us. They determined that André Sloga had just returned from vacation, and that he was attacked by a group of thieves who stole his luggage ... It's true that he lives in a pretty sketchy neighborhood ...

—In the paper, they said Rue Jeanne d'Arc ... That street's been cleaned up for several years now, it's almost become residential, and with the new library ...

He gathered from her pout and the way she wrinkled her nose that she did not share his point of view on the improved standing of this pocket of the 13th Arrondissement.

—Do you know if he can speak?

—I watched him for two hours, early this morning ... He experienced sudden bouts of terror, like anyone who comes in like that ... He yelled ...

—Were you able to understand any of it?

—No. Actually, he didn't yell, he didn't have the strength ... He murmured, but you could see that he was trying to yell. Then he calmed down and started to speak.

—What exactly did he say?

—Nothing. Disconnected words with no meaning …

Gabriel leaned toward her.

—What words? It's important … Try to remember, please.

She closed her eyes for a few moments.

—He said "loudspeaker" several times, yes, that's it … "the loudspeaker on the square …" That came back every ten minutes or so … He also repeated "the bank, the bank," and once, just once, he said a name …

Gabriel placed his hand over the young woman's.

—What name?

She looked at him square in the face.

—"Max."

4

THE REFRIGERATOR ARTISTS

"Max, the bank, the loudspeaker on the square ..." Gabriel left the Pitié-Salpêtrière, his head spinning like an old scratched record with the words the writer had spoken on his sickbed. "Max, the bank, the loudspeaker on the square." He got into his car and sat there for a moment, motionless, his elbows resting on the steering wheel, as he tried to figure out the magic combination that would be the key to the puzzle. *The bank of Max beneath the loudspeaker on the square. A max of banks for the crowd-speakers on the square. The proud speaker of Max's square. Speak loudly, Max, on the banks of the square* ... The roar of a train on the elevated tracks snapped him out of his reverie. He started the car and took off toward Rue Jeanne d'Arc, which he followed almost as far as Tolbiac. Before getting out, he took the precaution of shoving two pieces of licorice chewing gum that had been softening on his dashboard into his mouth and removing about twenty centimeters from a spool of orange mending thread.

The artists who'd been squatting in the neighborhood had pasted colorful hand-painted posters to walls and posts, and taped them to the windows of sympathetic shopkeepers. If you came close enough and spent a little time, it was possible to decipher the tormented calligraphy of the words, and to understand that they were protesting the imminent expulsion of a hundred painters, sculptors, and actors from the abandoned refrigeration warehouses that overlooked the train tracks, just steps from the Seine.

Gabriel walked up the street and found the name "André Sloga" among the labels on the intercom of the corner building. He knew the writer lived like a lone wolf, that he made no secret of a misogyny fueled by the failure of three marriages, but he pressed the button anyway to make sure the apartment was empty. He noted that by day, it was possible to enter the building's foyer by buzzing yourself in. On the other hand, a reinforced door prevented access to the rest of the building.

From the depths of his pocket, Gabriel dug out his "key to the city," a gift from the chief of the fire station on Rue de la Pompe. The master key could be used with any locking system, from the poorly jury-rigged to the most sophisticated, in all of Paris and the nearby suburbs. The twelve steel pins clicked in beautiful unison, like a regiment of ass-kissers who've stumbled upon a field marshal, and he found himself in a long, grey corridor with three rows of mailboxes along its right-hand wall.

André Sloga used two boxes: the first, fairly small, for letters, and another for bulkier pieces. Gabriel removed the advertisements that had also managed to cross the electronic barrier, and noticed that a dozen letters lay on the bottom of the first metal box. He checked to see that no one was coming from either direction, then unfurled the orange thread to its end, to which he attached the sticky brown mass he'd been kneading in his mouth for the last five minutes. He slid the gum into the box, jerking it this way and that in a fishing motion, then setting it down on top of the paper. He was careful to remoisten the sugary wad after each capture, and it took him less than a minute to remove all of the mail addressed to the writer. Seven notices concerning the finer points of domestic survival that end up draining the lifeblood from us all: Public Treasury, telephone, electricity, insurance. He sent them back into their void and kept only the four envelopes with no business name or return address. Then he attacked the box for parcels. The orange thread and licorice chewing gum had reached the limits of their combined powers. But the thin sheet-metal door bent beneath the pressure of his hands, and with the tip of his middle finger he was able to retrieve the single package, as thick as a pack of cigarettes, that lay at the bottom. The metal snapped back in place as soon as he let go. He tucked the letters and package under his belt and was about to leave the building when the clicking of the entrance door's steel pins resounded in the corridor. He grabbed a doorknob and found himself facing the trash chute. He didn't have the luxury of trying to find the stairwell a second time; the ceiling light had already caught his yellowing reflection on the polished skull of Inspector Vergeat. The pig let out a prolonged squeal. That was how he laughed.

—Lecouvreur! Unbelievable. Seriously, you're the last person I expected to run into here, but in fact, you're right at home.

—Am I? How do you mean?

—Yes, you're at home wherever it stinks of shit!

Vergeat had approached the battery of mailboxes and seemed reassured to find André Sloga's full.

He moved in a curious manner, repeatedly tugging at the creases in his pants, stroking his coat pockets, verifying at least thirty times the efficacious presence of the buttons on his shirt, the solidity of his belt buckle, the contents of his pocket. After each of their encounters, Gabriel vowed to describe Vergeat's behavior to an alcoholic psychiatrist who hung out at the Pied de Porc à la Sainte-Scolasse, but had never been able to follow up, as the shrink always seemed to have reached the limits of his ability to comprehend anything by the time the Octopus thought to bring it up. In reality, he didn't want to know too much about the calcified inner workings of the policeman; he wanted to keep the fight fair, without leaning on science. It wasn't Vergeat himself who was the enemy, but the cop inside the man.

—So, explain … What the fuck are you doing here?

Gabriel lifted a finger toward the floors above.

—Nothing. I came to visit my aging aunt …

The inspector shoved his hands into his pants pockets and massaged his thighs through the fabric.

—I didn't know this André Sloga was a faggot!

—I have no idea who you're talking about … Friend of yours? Someone who lives here?

Vergeat lifted his knees, one after the other, to pull up his socks.

—Don't play dumb with me, I might beat you at your own game … You know why I'm not surprised to find you here?

—Do tell.

—For the simple reason that you could have been his son! The same stew floats in both your hydrocephalic skulls ... Defiance of law and order, unmotivated hatred of uniforms, simplistic challenging of statute ... Pains in the ass, that's what you are. Congenital pains in the ass!

He punctuated his diatribe with a series of slaps to his coattails. Gabriel made a move toward the door. Vergeat rammed his shoulder against the wall.

—What are you doing in these parts? I'm still waiting for you to answer.

—Listen, inspector, I'm just an ordinary citizen, and like any ordinary citizen I'm free to walk where I see fit without having to explain myself to any authority, civilian or military ... On the other hand, I've got quite a few questions about you ...

Vergeat removed his glasses from their natural resting place and nervously wiped them with his handkerchief, which he smoothed and refolded neatly before putting it away.

—I'd be interested in hearing them ...

—What could an uncultivated pig like you understand about the life of a writer of Sloga's stature?

The inspector pulled himself onto the tips of his toes to dig his claws into Gabriel's jacket collar. The words hissed through his too-white teeth.

—You can't possibly know how much I hate guys like you ... Your sense of superiority makes me sick. It's not the only dream I have, but I swear, one day I will break you ...

All at once he became aware of the ridiculousness of his position. His fingers let go of the collar, and his heels regained contact with the hallway's tiled floor. He straightened his tie.

—I don't know what you're after, Lecouvreur, but you won't find anything ... We're tracking a gang of junkies who are squatting in the old warehouses of Austerlitz and pay for their fixes by attacking night owls in parking lots ... This isn't the first ...

—What's curious is that they would send you on such a job ... I wasn't aware that they'd created a surveillance squad for parking lots back at HQ ...

Vergeat restored the shine to his shoes by rubbing them on the backs of his pant legs.

—You yammer and yammer, and you don't know a tenth of what we've got. HQ is just the tip of the iceberg ... Everything happens at the lower levels. As soon as the name André Sloga was entered into the complaints database on the main computer, someone made the connection and his file was faxed to us ... He had us by the balls, this hack, in the 70s ... Big time! So they asked me to come take a look, as a formality, even though the stiff's shown no sign of life for almost a quarter of a century ... We don't like loose ends. It's that simple ...

The inspector frowned when Gabriel began to pull on the tails of his own jacket, to smooth out invisible creases.

—That's reassuring to hear ... He must have really given you hell ...

Gabriel fingered the flap of his pants fly, setting off a series of nervous tics on Vergeat's face and causing him to forget, momentarily, the state of his own apparel.

—A ton of it ... The worst was when he secretly moved

in with a Polynesian woman on a Pacific island in the middle of a nuclear test zone, near Moruroa … The military found out the night before H-Day, and they had to postpone the whole program …

Gabriel zipped and unzipped his fly twice, taking advantage of the inspector's embarrassment to make his way toward the door.

—I know this story: Sloga recounts it in detail in *Weekend at Nagasaki* … You can still find it at the used book stalls.

He backed away down the hall and pushed the button to exit. Before the door clicked shut, he saw Vergeat open André Sloga's mailboxes, using a skeleton key on a crowded key ring, and remove the bills.

5

TIED FOR FIRST PRIZE AT
THE YOUNG THEATER OF THE REAL

Gabriel ordered a pint at the bar of the Cantagrel. As he sifted through Sloga's letters, he watched Vergeat leave the building. The inspector had apparently not gone up to the writer's apartment, and Gabriel struggled against the desire to go himself. He decided to walk as far as the Tolbiac bridge as a means of forcing himself to think.

He had once been passionate about steel architecture, and he would certainly have become an engineer if the hardware store owned by his uncle Émile and aunt Marie-Claude, who raised him after the death of his parents, hadn't been located at the end of the Passage des Deux Soeurs, a hundred meters from a place called Block 18, where the skinheads met. Twice a day on his way to the university, he would pass the windows plastered with gothic posters for a hard-rock band, Commando 88, without paying them much attention—until the day when a prominent lawyer's son who'd become an active Autonomist, not out of rebellion against his family but out of conviction, explained the skinhead code of numbers to him: the "18" stood for "Adolf Hitler," the "1" for "A," the first letter in the alphabet, and the "8" for "H." The "88" was even more obvious: one "H" for "Heil" and the other for "Hitler." On top of that, if you scratched off two curves from each "8" you would get the acronym "S.S." The hardware store stocked all the resources necessary to launch a siege. The following week, two Molotov cocktails, perfectly dosed, shattered the front window of Block 18, and, as a bonus, set two Harley Davidsons on fire. A month later, after the upstanding people of the neighborhood had readily identified him and gone to the police, after his educational deferral from mandatory service had been rescinded, he found himself traipsing through the heart of a German forest buried in snow. Six months of military punishment that he made the best of by perfecting his knowledge of weaponry.

He leaned on the bridge's armature, near a cast-iron plaque that credited its design to the nineteenth-century engineer Daydé, and took the four letters from his pocket. The postmark on the first one indicated that it had been sent from Fontenay-sous-Bois five weeks earlier. He tore open the envelope and removed a sheet of paper covered in minuscule handwriting.

Fontenay, 24 July, 1995
Élisabeth Puchet
12, Rue Maxime Gorki
94 Fontenay-sous-Bois

Dear M. Sloga,

I pick up the pen anew, not knowing if my previous letters have reached you. I discovered this address (is it your address?) only after struggling for some time. None of your publishers seems to have preserved a relationship with you, and they claim to be incapable of making contact. By a happy accident, my brother works at the airport in Roissy for one of your cousins, and that has given me the means to write to you.

I direct a theater company that has already produced a number of original works drawn from major contemporary literary texts (*Blood and Misery* by Pierre Bondieff, and *The Impossible Reply* by Phillipe Duras, which tied for First Prize at the Young Theater of the Real, for example) and my dearest hope is to be able to stage an adaptation of the work that is, to my mind, your most successful: *Solace for the Hopeless* ...

Gabriel refolded the insufferable missive without taking the time to read to the end. The second letter came from an organization that distributed royalties to authors. André Sloga was to show up at the teller's window, on Rue Ballu, between nine o'clock and noon to retrieve the advance he had requested for a series of readings of some of his texts on a radio station in the overseas territories. The third envelope contained a monthly bill for photocopies, documents, and office supplies sent by Docutec, Inc. The surprise was hidden in a shabby manila envelope, un-stamped, the kind used only by the social-welfare services in the districts near the city limits. The message, drawn in capital letters on a sheet torn from an advertising pamphlet vaunting the merits of Corona beer, was impressive in its brusqueness:

FINAL WARNING

Gabriel turned the paper over several times before replacing it in its envelope.

The sole parcel did bear the address of its sender:

LOST & FOUND INK
Bibliographic research
33 Rue de la Santé, 75013 Paris

The book within was accompanied by a form letter thanking the client for the confidence he had placed in Lost & Found Ink. The book's cover was completely blank except for the name of an obscure publisher in Narbonne: Path and Terroir. It was a well-preserved volume from the early 1950s, with engravings embellishing the first page of each chapter. He read the title on the flyleaf: *The Five Senses* by Joseph Délteil. An interminable convoy of passing delivery trucks made the Tolbiac bridge shudder, and brought a burst of air that fluttered the pages he'd been leafing through. A paragraph caught his eye:

"Each hour, a shiny-faced pickaninny would come to ask after the women who were sick with chlamydia. Lines of Negresses, their tits in gourds …"

A hand came down suddenly on his shoulder as he was closing the book, stunned by the word *Negresses*. Inspector Vergeat brought his face close and yelled over the roar of the ancient trains.

—Interesting place to read!

Gabriel pointed at the four glass silos in the middle of

the no-man's-land of the development zone that Austerlitz
had become.

—You'd think so. But they've fallen behind in the construction of my library ...

He walked away without another word. The windshield of the Peugeot was adorned with a second ticket;
they seemed to proliferate in the 13th. He placed it on top of
the burgeoning pile that awaited the inaugural amnesty of
Chirac's second term, and headed for the Rue Popincourt.

As soon as he set foot on the tile floor of the salon,
the Yorkshire Terrier that belonged to the apprentice hairdresser ran toward him and flopped on its back, its four
legs quivering, and the fifth displaying its little lipstick. Gabriel tried to flip the dog back onto its paws with the tip
of his cowboy boot, but the beast's fur slid off the leather.
The customers laughed beneath their hair-dryers, and it
was clear from their expressions that they were all imagin-
ing what the proprietress's husband must have been doing
to the apprentice to put a pet as innocent as this in such a
state. Gabriel opened the door to the apartment and suc-
ceeded in banging it into the frantic dog's muzzle. Cheryl
was taking advantage of the relative lack of customers at
the end of the morning to take a break from the chatter of
the "Wigs," a categorical term that applied to all but two or
three of the salon's regulars. She was lounging on the window seat amidst her collection of stuffed animals, watching
a compilation of Marilyn Monroe's musical performances
for the thousandth time. He bent down to kiss her neck.
She propped herself up on her elbows, making her breasts
jut out.

—I get the sense your morning wasn't dull ...

—Not really ... What makes you say that?

She stretched a hand out toward his crotch.

—The magic shop's still open!

Gabriel quickly zipped up his fly.

—You don't need to worry. I was playing a joke on Vergeat ...

Cheryl pressed a button on the remote control to re-wind the tape.

—Really! I guess your relationship has taken a turn for the better ... Now you pass the time by taking off your pants? That's original ...

He sat next to her to recount the series of events that had occupied his morning, from the first parking ticket at Place Léon Blum to its twin sister on Rue Jeanne d'Arc.

When he finished, she was naked.

After that, the world existed only for others.

6

LOST & FOUND INK

Gabriel woke up alone in the middle of a family of kangaroos. The hair dryers were emitting an insistent whirr that drowned out the din of activity. He brushed aside the stuffed animals so he could gather up his clothes. He had returned from his adventure with the four letters addressed to André Sloga and the book by Joseph Délteil, which he turned back to now. Well before Camus, the plague had descended upon the world described in *The Five Senses*. Everyone was trying desperately to get to the north pole, where the virus apparently lost its potency. Élie-Élie, Scientist of the State, became the sacrificial lamb. As he labored to save the world, each of the five senses the Creator, in his largesse, had offered to Man were torn away from him, one by one, like five exploding flowers: Hearing, Smell, Taste, Sight, Touch.

Gabriel, a savvy reader of detective novels, detected the stink in Élie-Élie as soon as he appeared beneath the delicate pen of Joseph Délteil.

"He was born in Vienna (Austria) to a Yid, but with an American mother."

He stopped for a moment on the compensatory "but,"

which multiplied the sentence's loathsomeness, before reading on:

The two kinds of blood, Jewish and Yankee, were
as harmonious in his veins as they were in society.
To their mingling, he owed his facial features and
his business sense. Viennese waltzes, Esau's lentils,
and Chicago-style pork all contributed, with their
complementary forms of nourishment, to his weak
and fleshy soul. He was delicate like an archduke
and fat like a Wall Street banker.

Nausea overcame him well before the end of this portrait, but he forced himself to read every disgusting word.

A kind of millennial force, coated with music and
fat, emanated from his greasy corpulence, from his
face with its gold-rimmed glasses. This flower—a
monstrous eunuch, a hybrid beauty—united, in his
person, old Slavonic flesh with brand-new bones:
Moses and Rockefeller.

Gabriel let the volume slide from his hands and remained motionless for a while, his gaze tilted toward the
ceiling as he concocted a number of scenarios, each as un-
satisfying as the last, to explain the presence of such a piece
of work in the mailbox of a man like André Sloga. It made
no sense. He went downstairs, poking his cowboy boot into
the Yorkie's hindquarters before the door to the salon was
even fully open. The miniature canine squealed all the way

to his mistress's station and took refuge under a sink. As he passed, Gabriel quickly kissed Cheryl, who was busy giving a perm to the actress who played Jackie Sardou in the Sound and Light show. Up the street, the car was receiving the distinction of yet another parking infraction.

The offices of Lost & Found Ink consisted of a garret with an ancient fanlight, on the eighth floor of a building with no elevator. Gabriel hadn't been back to the neighborhood around the Santé municipal prison since the glory days when students had assembled there to demonstrate against a minimum wage law proposed by the last right-wing minister of a president who claimed to be on the left. The disparate protesters had joined together and were rushing the high walls, pursued by National Guardsmen eager for some action, when the detainees grabbed the bars of their cells and yelled out to the demonstrators that the cars parked on Rue de la Santé belonged to the wardens. Throughout the year, this little corner of Parisian paradise was given a pass by the meter maids, and those men and women who'd been sentenced to life, whose only mental stimulation came from the activity in the neighborhood, had forgotten what a parking ticket looked like. The protesters made a quick job of overturning the Peugeot GTIs, the Renault TSs, the Citroën ZXs, and Mercedes TDs that were being paid off in monthly installments with the bitter sweat of the condemned. Gabriel had restricted himself to helping the kids set fires, out of a fear of being mistaken, at his age, for an infiltrating cop.

Now he bowed his head and took a half step into the offices of Lost & Found Ink, pushing lightly on the door, which had been left ajar to let in an illusory current of air. The floor creaked, attracting the attention of a man of about sixty who was stuffing books into generic envelopes similar to the one addressed to André Sloga. His face glistened with perspiration, and beads of sweat, heavy like the first drops in a storm, splashed onto book covers, bills, and packages. He looked up, pausing to wipe his forehead with his shirt sleeve.

—What do you want?

Gabriel ignored the question.

—Are you the person who searches for hard-to-find books?

—If one wants to earn a living in this racket, one quickly discovers that it's better to find the books for which people are searching …

Gabriel indicated, with a slight movement of his features, that this demonstration of wit had not gone unnoticed. As he approached, he read several titles from the spines of books piled up next to the postage meter. *The Beetles of Andalusia* by Jaime Izquierdo, *The Wind in the Trenches* by Francois Dubanchet, *Wine and Spirituality* by Robert Illier … He didn't know exactly how to engage with this strange and damp man, who was continuing to make up packages. Not being suspicious by nature, Gabriel decided to start by playing it straight.

—Do you know André Sloga?

The man paused for a moment and then stuffed an

envelope with *Letters to a friend who is dead and gone* by Clotilde Tempruns, the cover of which was decorated with a scarlet band advertising that this tome had been awarded the Valentine-Abraham-Verlain Prize, given by the Academie Française to a "poetess visited by unhappiness."

—Certainly ... People ask for him from time to time. In fact, I believe all of his books are out of print, and none of them went into paperback editions ... Though there are some that deserve to ... What title are you looking for?

Gabriel positioned himself below the fanlight, which allowed him to stand up a bit straighter.

—None of them ... I have all of his books at home ... I'm helping him a little with his research ... I type his manuscripts ...

—He's still writing?

—He was writing ...

The man stopped mid-gesture and lifted his head, surprised.

—What do you mean, "He was writing"? I didn't know he'd died.

—He hasn't, yet ... You haven't heard about what happened? It was in this morning's *Parisien* ...

—If you think I have time to waste reading newspapers ...

Gabriel withdrew a sheet of notebook paper covered with notes he'd taken while reading *The Five Senses* from his pocket. He unfolded it as if it were a precious document.

—He had a fairly serious accident while getting out of his car ... I've just come from the hospital, and he's asked me for all sorts of things ... It's a crazy list. There are things on it I don't even understand!

This allusion to mystery whet the curiosity of the rare-book hunter, whose eyes lit up.

—What kinds of things?

Gabriel refolded the paper meticulously and slid it into his pocket.

—I won't bother you with that; I'll manage ... As far as you're concerned, he asked me to draw up a list of all the books he's ordered from you ... He can only remember the last one, by Délteil ...

The finder of unfindable things opened the top drawer of his desk to remove an imposing black register with a gold edge, which he consulted, wetting the tip of his index finger with his tongue.

—Délteil! Joseph or Gérard? You must specify, there are many Délteils now.

—It was Joseph ... An odd little book ...

He smoothed down a page with the palm of his hand.

—Voilà! André Sloga, 2 Rue Jeanne d'Arc ... This will go quickly: his first request, by mail, was three months ago ... He began with *The Rubble* by Lucien Rebatet, *Fascist Socialism* and *With Doriot* by Drieu la Rochelle, the second edition of the *Nouvelle Révue Française* from 1943 with a dedication from the author to the chief of the special delegation for Saint-Denis. He then got *Trifles for a Massacre* by Louis-Ferdinand Céline, and last month I sent him the Path and Terroir reissue of *The Five Senses* by Joseph Délteil.

Gabriel was dumbfounded.

—Thank you ... Do people often request these sorts of books?

The bookseller in the garret could not repress a satisfied smile.

—More and more ... These are authors who are coming back into vogue.

7

SERBO-BOSNIO-CROATO-SLOVENES

From the sentry booth in front of the hospital, a clone in a familiar white shirt was busy screening the crowd of visitors, and Gabriel crossed the pavilions of the Pitié unimpeded all the way to the library. Balanced on a small aluminum stepladder with a feather duster in her hand, the well-read nurse was swiping gently at the tops of the shelves, which bowed beneath the weight of masses of tattered books. Her outstretched arms caused the back of her smock to rise, revealing a sizable portion of her thighs, still bronzed from a recent summer holiday. Gabriel enjoyed the show for the time it took her to dust two meters worth; then, suddenly conscious of a presence, she spun around and tugged futilely at the bottom of her smock.

—Hello …

She remained perched on the ladder, the feather bouquet aimed at the ceiling, her eyes exactly level with Gabriel's.

—Hello … I was passing by, and I stopped to see if there was any news about André Sloga.

She rested her elbow between two volumes of the Petit Robert dictionary.

—The news is good ... At least, better ... He left intensive care early this afternoon, and he's in the trauma unit now, resting ...

—Do the doctors have a prognosis?

—From what I've heard, none of the damage is irreversible. He's sturdy for his age. It will take some time for his constitution to recover. On the other hand ...

She paused. Gabriel chewed the inside of his cheek.

—On the other hand?

—The projections are more reserved when it comes to the effects of the attack on his psychological state.

—What does that mean, exactly?

—We have plenty of examples of victims who are fine physically, but who refuse to reintegrate into the harsh reality of the world. They refuse by way of aphasia, amnesia, madness ... Your friend is showing all of the symptoms of this phenomenon.

Gabriel shook his head.

—Do you think it might be possible for me to see him?

—Not officially, but he's in the Galbérine wing, on the second floor. If you take the service elevator you won't have to pass reception ... You didn't hear it from me.

She waved goodbye from her ladder with the feather duster.

Two West Indian orderlies were arguing about the civil war in Yugoslavia, one accusing the Serbo-Bosnians and Serbo-Croatians of ethnic cleansing, rape, and summary executions, and the other charging the Bosnian Serbs and the Croato-Slovenes with the same evils. Gabriel waited for a moment next to an ambulance, ducking into the freight elevator as soon as the echoes of the argument moved away down the corridor. He tripped over the mountains of dirty linens that sat in piles on the second floor, regaining his balance thanks to a fire extinguisher that nearly detached from the wall under the force of his weight.

He almost passed by André Sloga without recognizing him. The writer's forehead had disappeared beneath bandages that blended into the white of the pillowcase, setting off his profile and the sunken depths of his eye sockets. He lifted the lids of his unmistakable silver eyes just as Gabriel was opening the door to the next ward over. After making sure no one was watching, he retraced his steps and went to crouch between the raised bed and the bedside table, which was covered in meds. He took the old man's right hand in his, hoping to attract his attention.

—Monsieur Sloga, can you hear me? Monsieur Sloga ... André ...

After twenty of these tender caresses, Gabriel was rewarded with a sleepy groan. He wouldn't be discouraged. Much later, after he had ducked down three times to evade the trained eyes of the floor wardens, a few scattered syllables began to punctuate the moaning. Gabriel straightened up enough to place his ear next to Sloga's lips, while continuing to stroke his bony hand. The syllables became more numerous, then regrouped themselves to form words: "Square, loudspeaker, Max ..." The same words the librarian had reported to him earlier that morning. Gabriel was preparing to accept the fact that this second visit was useless, when Sloga articulated a near-complete sentence.

—It's Max, on the loudspeaker, the square ...

It was as if the effort he'd expended to recall a semblance of grammatical logic had exhausted his last resources, for Sloga fell immediately into a deep torpor. Gabriel replaced the writer's hand on the sheet and left, after giving him one last look.

The Peugeot was parked at the intersection of Jenner and Esquirol, in the neighborhood where the city's shrinks have their offices, and Gabriel disposed of his third offense of the day Paris-style: with his windshield wipers. A police car was parked in front of 2 Rue Jeanne d'Arc, forcing him to abandon, for the moment, his plan to visit the writer's apartment. He headed slowly back up toward the metro station at Nationale and found himself in front of Notre-Dame de la Gare, the only church in the capital designed by a railroad architect. He had seen photos of the nave, its form inspired by vast waiting rooms.

The sign on the corner copy shop drew his attention away from the monument: Docutec. He rifled through his pockets and took out one of the envelopes he'd fished out of André Sloga's mailbox; it contained a bill for photocopies and office supplies totaling one hundred thirty-seven francs. His memory hadn't deceived him: the logo and the sign matched. He pushed open the door to the store. A young trainee of about fifteen was loading a ream of paper into the Rank Xerox. She greeted him while bending down to lower the block of paper into one of the machine's drawers. Gabriel unfolded the bill and placed it on the counter, between the Lettraset display and the Pilot pens, along with a two-hundred-franc note. She stamped "Paid" beneath the total before clumsily giving him his change. She blushed when he pointed out that there were ten francs missing from the change tray.

—I don't have the hang of this yet ... I'm here for two weeks, just until classes pick up again ... I started at the beginning of the week ...

He slid the two-tone coin toward himself and was about to make the mistake of asking for the manager so he could question him about André Sloga when, the bill in one hand, the student-employee turned to a series of filing cabinets that lined a portion of the wall, each marked with a letter of the alphabet. Her free hand stopped on the card marked *S* and pulled out a shopping bag from Gallimard Jeunesse decorated with an apple cut into quarters, which she handed to him with a smile.

—Here you are, Monsieur Sloga. I hope you're happy with it ...

Gabriel was unable to hide his surprise. Words came to his rescue.

—A few more minutes and I'd have completely forgotten! See how you've distracted me ...

He distanced himself quickly from the shop, expecting at each step to be called back by the owner emerging from his stockroom. It wasn't until he was seated at the wheel, in the shelter of the Peugeot, that he opened the bag. A diskette in a plastic sleeve was taped to a cardboard box containing about a hundred sheets of paper covered in impeccable typescript. A title, in blocky, shadowed capital letters, extended to the edges of the flyleaf: *MOON OVER THE MARSHES*.

YOLANDA OF THE MARSHES

Gabriel Lecouvreur had installed himself at the back of the Pied de Porc to read what appeared to be André Sloga's manuscript-in-progress while drinking a bottle of Tinchebray Amber, brewed in the Orne by someone vaguely related to André Breton.* Gérard prowled around the leatherette booth, sweeping up the floor, wiping down neighboring tables, cleaning the mirrors. He would peek at a few words over Gabriel's bony shoulder as he passed, then find another pretext to return to his close proximity. Exasperated, Gabriel threw the sheets of paper down on the Formica before beginning the eighth chapter.

—Could I read in peace for five minutes! What's with you, circling me like that since I got here!

The restaurateur pulled up a chair.

—Don't be annoyed … Is that by the guy you were talking about this morning? The one who got thrashed …

—Exactly. And I have the strong impression that what's written here is not unrelated to Sloga's attack.

Gérard leaned in.

—The Tinchebray: is it good? How do you like it?

* André Breton was from the Orne region of France.

—It's dry ...

—But what else?

Gabriel took a swallow to refresh his memory.

—I would say it's better than the pale Mora from Bonifacio that you served me last week, but it doesn't hold a candle to the Micheline-Lambic from Clermont-Ferrand ...

—You've always been unfair to the Corsicans ...

—It's Freudian. My mother was originally from Baraglioli, a godforsaken hole near Sartène ...

—That only half surprises me ... But what makes you think that what you're reading explains the attack on your guy?

Gabriel skimmed the last lines of the unfinished manuscript and downed the final dregs of his beer from Orne before responding.

—Do you remember the murder of that nurse from Fontenay-le-Comte?

Gabriel scratched his head.

—Vaguely ... Very vaguely, really ... And it was all over the papers at the time ... How long ago was that? Five years?

—Something like that ... Sloga has used it as the basis for his novel. The hypothesis he's come up with to explain the murder damned well holds its own, at least in the realm of fiction ...

Gérard signaled for him to wait and returned to the bar, bringing back two Micheline-Lambics and a saucer filled with salted peanuts and pistachios.

—Because I know you love them ... And what's the nature of his explanation?

—First of all, you have to remember that the murderer

of this woman, who in the book is called Yolanda, was never identified ... The Poitiers police arrested and incarcerated a wild coypu breeder from Maillezais who they were forced to let go, a year later, when the charges against him came to nothing ...

Gérard popped some nuts into his mouth.

—I remember the broad strokes, but the rest is a total blank ... Coypus, I remember that, now that you mention it ... They're river rats, right? Like beavers—they do things with their tails ...

Gabriel ignored the double entendre. He guzzled his Clermontian beer until not a drop was left, all the while admiring the consistent creaminess of the foam.

—The story is quite simple. At least at first glance ... One morning in October, a peasant from the marshes who has taken a boat out into his fields discovers a woman's body in a small channel at the end of the Bonvix river. Right away the body is identified as Yolanda's ... No, that's the name Sloga gave her ... She had a different name ...

—Keep it, makes it easier ...

—It'll come back to me ... Yolanda is the daughter of an industrialist in Fontenay-le-Comte: metal fabrication, vinyl windows, architectural ironwork ... A man of importance to the whole region, who provides factory jobs to a good half of the male population of the cantons of Maillezais and Bonvix ... At first, the police determined that the young woman was killed by multiple stab wounds to the heart, and they arrested a vagrant—an agricultural day laborer and borderline imbecile who admitted that the Laguiole knife found after days of dredging the nearby swamps was his.

And this was before the judge had even established that it was the presumed murder weapon ...

Gérard spit out some half-chewed pistachio.

—Is that some kind of joke? Seems to me it's difficult to "establish that it was the presumed murder weapon" ... If it's being "established," that means it's bogus!

—Precisely ... The farm worker languished in the clink for eleven months on the basis of a jurist's conclusions that were unfounded from start to finish ... Luscious Yolanda didn't die from the spectacular array of knife wounds tattooed on her chest; she had simply been strangled, then stabbed after the fact ... *Post mortem* ...

—And why? Some kind of nut job who finally lost it completely?

—No. According to Sloga, the point was to make it look like a burglary ... A year later, the investigation was assigned to a judge from Niort who deigned to make the trip to Bonvix only once. He didn't want to get his hands dirty. The whole thing was stalled indefinitely, and to this day Yolanda's real murderer runs free.

The Pakistani man who'd come in while Gabriel was talking had managed to sell his jasmine flowers to three couples seated in the back of the restaurant. Before leaving, he tucked a small, fragrant bouquet into the vase of roses Maria had placed on the end of the counter. Gérard gestured his thanks, then tapped the manuscript.

—It's a classic story ... Rustic setting, stagnant waters, innocent vagabond, impotent justice ... I can understand why a writer would be interested, but I don't see why a squad of commandos would come down from the swamps of Poitiers to prevent Sloga from writing a novel inspired by poor Yolanda's murder!

—I had the same reaction, at first ... I'm going to read you a bit of text, and you'll soon change your mind.

Gabriel leafed through the manuscript and stopped on a passage he'd underlined in pencil during his first reading.

—Listen:

They entered the farmyard. An old man's hovel with a chicken coop, rabbit hutch, woodshed, and duck pond. In the kitchen garden, near the leeks, cabbage, and potatoes, were a group of magnificent rose bushes and a large flowering magnolia. But the house itself was ugly and depressing, an ancient crumbling thing, patched up by its inhabitant, with walls that leaned like the tower of Pisa, and improvised gutters.

The interior was dismal and smelled of dust, old blankets, and cold ashes.

—Well, here you are! said Fernand. You haven't been here before ...?

—Never, said Yolanda.

—Can we call each other *tu*?

—Gladly ...

She set her satchel on the heavy kitchen table, opened it, and sat on the bench to prepare her instruments.

—Pull down your pants, please ...

Fernand turned around. His belt had ceased to hold in his belly. Yolanda lowered his underwear,

revealing a fleshy, varicose rump. The alcohol-
soaked cotton ball delineated a circle the size of a
five-franc coin, in the center of which she injected
the deadly poison. Fernand didn't flinch. He turned,
pants still around his knees, his sex roused, partially
erect and pointing toward the nurse.

Gabriel put the manuscript down.

—What do you think of it?

The owner of the Pied de Porc à la Sainte-Scolasse
dunked his lips in the thick foam of the Micheline-Lambic.
He clicked his tongue, an expression of pleasure on his lips.

—I think you have a knack for stopping the moment
things are getting interesting ...

—Give me your opinion instead of joking around. I
honestly want to know what it is you find interesting ...

—You're kidding, right? When he turns around and
hoists his flag ... You don't find that interesting?

They had known each other for ten years, and Gabriel
was very fond of Gérard: he was a faithful friend he knew he
could count on in his darkest moments. But he was forced
to acknowledge that the quantity of platitudes and inanity
that gushed forth on a regular basis from Gérard's clientele
was beginning to clog his neurons.

—I'm sorry to disappoint you, but what struck me
about the passage is this: "The alcohol-soaked cotton ball
delineated a circle the size of a five-franc coin, in the center
of which she injected *THE DEADLY POISON.*"

—That kind of thing, S&M, it just doesn't sink in with
me ... In bed, just like at the stove, I've still a hopeless

traditionalist ... Pig's feet prepared the classic way; mission-
ary position ...

—Have you lost it, or are you not following me on
purpose?

Gabriel gathered up the first pages of the manuscript
while Gérard went to ask the cook, Vlad, to take over at
the bar. Vlad was an imposing, taciturn Romanian originally from Cioranu, a sinister region on the Moldavian
border. Gérard only rarely put him behind the bar because
he was militantly opposed to the consumption of alcohol,
and when serving the customers he would mutter damn-
ing words between his teeth, which were as broad as spades.
The boss came back to take his place next to his friend.

—I need pedagogical guidance. Go ahead, I'm lis-
tening ...

—It couldn't be simpler ... André Sloga's little book
opens with the discovery of Yolanda's body, the arrest of
the vagabond by the Bonvix police, and the burial of the
victim ... It's written as straight as a die, a provincial drama,
a bit in the manner of Maupassant ... Here, just a few lines
and you'll understand Sloga's genius ... This is how he de-
scribes the arrival of distant cousins to the cemetery. It's
as if you're right there: "The villagers, too, cast them side-
long glances. The couple had the feeling they were being
spied on. The woman wore a loose-fitting jacket with a
small synthetic-fur collar and had her hands in her pockets. She was unsteady on her feet, like someone who had
been traveling since dawn. Next to her, the man seemed tall,
with a clean-shaven face, wide shoulders, a flat stomach, and
well-groomed russet-colored hair, slightly rumpled from

the journey." Four sentences, and you're part of the family! It's good, right?

—I'm with you, Gabriel. In any case, it's how I like my literature, "slightly rumpled from the journey" ...

—Me too. After that, the whole thing, at least what I've been able to read of it, is laid out as a succession of flashbacks. They are fairly short scenes, all structured in practically the same manner: Sloga establishes a character and his surroundings, then has Yolanda burst into his life and push him to his limits. She teases him mercilessly and refuses to put out, unless it will serve her better than would prolonging his sexual frustration ...

—A genuine bitch!

—That would be too simple. This isn't Robbe-Grillet.

Gérard cast a surreptitious look at his Moldavian cook.

—Don't dismiss detective novels, Gabriel, I liked *The Erasers* ...

Gabriel responded only with a disdainful shrug.

—As you've surely figured out, Yolanda works as an independent nurse in Bonvix. She knows every rear end in the region and can identify them by touch ... There are a few among them that she makes full use of: those of the pharmacist, the two doctors, the veterinarian, and a surgeon from Fontenay-le-Comte who comes to spend weekends at his family home. Everyone knows about her amorous tendencies, and throughout the county she has a solid reputation for nymphomania ...

—That seems rather unfair. What strikes me is her remarkable faithfulness to the medical corps ...

Gabriel ignored the wise crack, amusing as it was, and persevered:

—Fernand, who had you so worked up a moment ago, tried his luck because of the rumors, but Yolanda just patted him sweetly on the tip of his prick before packing up her gear. Basically, she only slept with them if it was useful. In a dozen chapters, we watch her inject the deadly virus into the immune systems of Fernand, the five doctors, and others of their ilk ...

Gérard's eyes opened wide.

—Oh, I see! The virus ... I hadn't realized that she's giving them AIDS! I see why she'd get herself bumped off! Which one of them figured it out first?

—That's the whole problem! It could be one of the six, or a plot between them all, like in Agatha Christie's *Ten Little Indians* ... Or like in Délteil's *Five Senses*, with Élie-Élie ... The Plague ... AIDS ...

—You've lost me now.

The Octopus pursued his train of thought without concern for his friend.

—Unless it came from outside. Only André Sloga has the answer, or rather, *had* the answer ... His brain has been soaking in sauerkraut since his *brétonnade*, and now he only says a few words: *Max, loudspeaker, bank,* and *square!* Even Columbo would eat his hat.

—There isn't anyone named Max in the manuscript?

Gabriel turned the bottle of Clermont upside down. A single auburn drop did him the favor of rolling from its neck.

—You've really been reading too much junk, haven't you? Some hack trots out a bunch of pop psychology and stock characters, and the marketplace claps its hands and asks for more ... You don't think it was the first thing I checked? ... I even went deeper into the hypothesis ... No Maxime, Masque, Lebanc, Laban, Loew, Speaker ... Nothing, not the least mention of any of them!

The cafe owner racked his brains for a way to save face.

—My job is to design dishes and cocktails; to marry flavors, colors; to harmonize for the eyes, the nose, the palate ... Not to analyze, dissect, perform autopsies ... That's your job! I'm partial to things invented by nature, not by man ... And in your story there are two things that give me pause: First, I honestly wonder why this young girl enjoys killing the medical personnel of the Poitiers swamps in such a ghastly manner. There must be a reason. And second, I cannot understand what would cause the daughter of a good family, whose father's got half the region under his thumb, to adopt the prosaic profession of independent nursing! It's the lowliest rank in medicine. Those kids are usually set up as dentists at least: from what I hear, that's a specialty that requires no more rigorous training than wholesale butchery does.

Gabriel put the manuscript back in its folder and placed the floppy disk on top.

—Congratulations, I arrived at the same conclusions. For the first question, I'm leaning heavily toward the theory of vengeance. I have a hunch that young Yolanda is picking off Bonvix's health professionals according to a meticulously developed plan. Fernand has his ass pricked for a nervous problem; the pharmacist is subject to spasms, one of the doctors to asthma, the other to allergies; the vet has a bad case of psoriasis, and the surgeon is addicted to morphine ... The why of the thing completely escapes me. But if it turns out she chose the profession of nursing from the start just so she could execute her plan, I'll leave you to imagine the weight she'd be carrying on her shoulders! The men who killed her were hell-bent on keeping their secret from being revealed ... The fact that Sloga is now a vegetable at the Pitié-Salpêtrière can only mean that he ferreted it out.

—If I know you, you'll be going to take a look around the marshes.

Gabriel stood up, the manuscript under his arm.

—I'm going to stop by Weston's, buy myself a good pair of waders, and I'm off!

9

RIVER RATS

Gabriel exited the Aquitaine highway just as the nine o'clock news began to air on France-Inter. He stopped at the public telephones across from a tollbooth. The apprentice with the Yorkie picked up, holding a blow dryer in her other hand. She told him, her sharp voice piercing through the din, that Cheryl had left an hour early to do the grocery shopping. The little beast yapped at her feet, as if signaled by a sixth sense that the object of his desire was on the line.

—Can you tell her I had to leave town, and that I won't be back until tomorrow or the next day?

He heard a small cry from the receiver and thought for a minute that she'd burned herself by putting the hairdryer to her ear instead of the telephone, but it was only a protestation from the Wig whose fate she held in her hands.

He followed the Sèvre Niortaise river for about ten kilometers, crossing sleepy villages dotted with houses, low-lying as if crushed by the weight of the past and tradition. Stocky peasants traveling on foot turned to look at the Peugeot as it passed, scanning the numbers and letters on the license plate for an explanation of the evening intrusion.

Bonvix distributed its dullness equally on both sides of the river. The church, the town hall, and the Agricultural

Credit Union occupied the heart of the large village, and at its base, the main street was interrupted by a narrow stone bridge that meant a long wait for cars coming from downriver. Copper plaques engraved with the names of attorneys, notaries public, and doctors gleamed in the electric glow of faux gas lamps, while the neon alternative of the pharmacy's sign cast a cold light on the charmless facades. Gabriel drew nearer to the edge of the village. The houses became more spaced out, shorter, and sadder, until they resembled Fernand's hovel as Sloga had described it in his manuscript. The water level was low; the wooden fishing boats sat half-exposed on the sludgy riverbed. An odor of stale dirt, spongy grasses, and fish rose from the trench, wafting into the car through the open window. He thought he made out the shadow of a giant rat on the road, just as the sign for the River Rat Inn came into view.

The parking lot, carved out of a field bordered by gorse bushes, abutted a cluster of small outcroppings used by anglers. He entered the inn. The main room seemed to have been hollowed out from the earth, and he had to stoop while descending the three massive steps to avoid smacking his head on the oak joists. The fifteen or twenty people, mostly men, who were seated at a bar constructed from logs fell silent and watched him for a long moment while, bowing slightly, he crossed the room to the small reception desk. It was distinguished only by the required list of room rates and a pegboard hung with keys.

The proprietor herself was a swamp thing: the honeycombed nose of an amphibian, thick skin and mustache, globular eyes, heavy breath, stubby limbs ... She brusquely described a room that looked out over the coppice, and he accepted it sight unseen before sitting down, without en- thusiasm, to a grey slab of freshwater fish pâté. He ordered a local beer, a pale Angle, which was served plain, without the detestable slice of poorly-rinsed lemon or moldy olive Parisian waiters habitually tossed in. The sad appearance of the pâté turned out to be misleading; the blandness of the tench, roach, and pike was fortuitously countered by a deli- cate balance of aromatic herbs, and he valiantly attacked the chanterelle omelet that followed. When he went upstairs to his room an hour later, the customers were still leaning their elbows on the logs. He bid them goodnight, but none of them responded.

His first visit, the next morning, was to the pharmacist. He looked nothing like the portrait Gabriel had sketched of him in his imagination: rachitic and sickly, observing the world from behind glasses perched on the tip of his nose, dragging his infected carcass back and forth across a coun- ter lined with bottles and potions. This apothecary had the physique of a butcher: a portly torso, hands like frying pans, prominent cheekbones, and a straightforward gaze, which met that of the detective. The Octopus stammered out a request for aspirin. The pharmacist slid the box out from a paper bag emblazoned with a red cross and handed over his change. Gabriel took two steps toward the exit, then turned around.

—Excuse me, but have you been here a long time?
The man's lips curled into a smile tinged with irony.
—Why do you ask? Got your eyes on the place …
—No, I'm as incompetent at real estate as I am at

pharmacopoeia ... It's just that I was a journalist once, and I followed the story of Valérie Audiat, that young woman who was found next to a small lock in the swamp ...

The reference to the crime made the man suspicious. His eyes hardened.

—It's been talked about much too much, blathered about all over ... People here would rather forget it ... The press did a lot of damage.

Gabriel shoved the medication into his pocket.

—Those are some of the reasons I changed professions ... I was a journalist, but ... Now I edit and revise manuscripts ... Peace and quiet are what I need. I remembered the area, and I said to myself that at the end of the season, it would be the ideal ...

—For quiet, you can't do better: with the amount of sleeping pills and antidepressants I sell, there's no chance of a crisis within a radius of twenty kilometers! I imagine that with what ends up going into the waste water, even the fish are getting treated for their blues.

Gabriel wrinkled his brow to show that he was thinking.

—I actually think that I came into your pharmacy for an interview at the time, but I can't put a face on the person who was here in your place ...

—You won't have a chance to see it again, except in a photo ... I took over for him four years ago. He was very sick, and he died a few months later ...

Gabriel leaned in toward the pharmacist.

—What did he die of, if I'm not being too indiscreet?

—Here, when we speak of it, we call it swamp fever.

10

TO DOC OR NOT TO DOC

Gabriel walked along the dock from which the flat-bottomed fishing boats, loaded up with the year's last tourists, flooded the canals of the hinterland. For the length of a summer, perpetually unemployed men of a certain age were able to escape their government-subsidized lives by plunging long boathooks into the slimy depths. They braced themselves on the wooden handles, their bodies cantilevered over the water, and then propelled the skiffs forward with a single thrust of the pelvis, marking their paths with the tips of their poles on the river's surface. Children scoured the banks for coypus; the women smiled, happy; and the men, their eyes glued to point-and-shoots and camcorders, immortalized their cropped version of reality in video and film. Back on the square, a young woman with a headful of curls and the profile of a sheep was attempting to unlock the door to the veterinarian's office. Gabriel watched for a moment before approaching her.

—Would you like some help?

She turned around, and he noticed that she was slightly less ugly from the front than from the side. She handed him the crowded key ring.

—Yes, that would be nice ... I don't understand it at all, it only works half the time ...

He looked at the nearly identical keys one by one, bending down to examine the mechanism itself. He tried a different key from the one the woman had been struggling with, and the cylinder turned effortlessly. She took a perfume-soaked handkerchief from her bag and pressed it to her nose and mouth, then entered the waiting room, the walls of which were adorned with cheap posters of cats, dogs, birds, and tortoises. A layer of dust obscured the covers of the old magazines that blanketed the floor. A rank, composite odor, like what trails in the wake of less than meticulous taxidermists, seemed to have been deposited in several distinct layers throughout the room. Every movement revealed more of its nauseating variety. Though he had wisely remained at the doorstep, Gabriel recoiled, suffocating.

—My God! It's like being at a morgue during a strike!

The young woman with the graceless profile had crossed the room to open the two windows, holding her breath. She rejoined Gabriel on the sidewalk to air out her clothing and hair. She was breathing laboriously through her handkerchief. He wrinkled his nose.

—So, where does that stink come from?

She smiled to show that she understood what he was referring to.

—The vet I'm supposed to be replacing has been dead for a month ...

—In my humble opinion, it's high time to remove the body, or else it will be weeks before the stench subsides ...

Her smile broadened.

—Don't worry, he was at the hospital when it happened ... The problem is that he didn't have an assistant, and everything was left as it was ... The odor comes from the freezer ... It was full to the brim with dead animals that need to be removed by special services, and the electrical company had the brilliant idea to cut off the juice! I had a feeling it wouldn't be easy to move to Bonvix, but this, this is something ...

—Where are you from?

—Rueil-Malmaison. I'd had enough of doggie-dogs and kitty-cats ...

—I understand completely. My wife also takes care of hairy beasts, and it gets to her more than it should ...

—That's funny! You're married to a vet?

—No, a hairdresser.

She leaned on his arm and collapsed in laughter. He pointed toward the minuscule terrace of the only bar in Bonvix, the Gantua, which was across from the disused train station.

—Can I offer you a coffee, while the air clears?

She glanced at her watch.

—The main thing is I can't miss the corpse collectors. They'd better not be late ...

—We'll see them arrive. We won't be able to miss them from there.

They settled in at one of the two tables exposed to the timid midmorning sun and, instead of coffee, ordered two pale Angle beers, which arrived tainted with oozing slices of lemon that the barman, with an air of self-satisfaction, had slotted on the mugs' rims. Gabriel lifted his glass, after relieving it of the unwelcome intrusion.

—To your new job!

They let the foam dissolve on their lips. Gabriel knew enough to shut up, but he didn't have to for long; the young woman quickly picked up the conversation.

—Are you on vacation in the area?

—No. For that I would need the sea, palm trees, coral reefs, and for everyone to be speaking Creole, at least ... I'm just getting some country air. I work for a publisher, revising manuscripts, improving novelists' prose, strengthening sentences, toning paragraphs, sculpting chapters ... You could call me a "professor of literary fitness" ...

—I think that's something I would love ...

Gabriel played it cool.

—It's frustrating more than anything else ... You can't imagine what it's like to watch a guy whose sinking book you saved swagger all over the stage of a literary television show, and blush with pleasure while the host of the day flatters the quality of his style! I've had future winners of the Goncourt in my hands ... If I read you the original, you would think I was making it up ...

—I had no idea that's how it worked ...

—Oh! It's the same in every profession. For example in your field, medicine ... A whole team works for years on a virus, and when the vaccine is discovered everyone says it's Professor Blank's vaccine, not the vaccine created by Professor Blank and his team. There's only one name on the nomination form for the Nobel Prize: *Dr. Blank*, period, done! Anyway. How did he die, your predecessor?

She looked at him, amused.

—Why do you ask me that?

—For my own protection ... Yesterday, I had a sore

throat, and I went to see the pharmacist. He's new too ... The one before him keeled over from swamp fever, from what I've heard. If that's the same thing that got your veterinarian, I'd want to take some precautions ...

She lifted her arm to order a second round of Angles and lowered her voice as soon as the waiter had turned his back.

—You're right, they both died from the same illness, but it has nothing to do with the swamp ...

—What was it?

She leaned closer.

—AIDS ... No one dares speak the word ...

—AIDS! That's no joke. I've heard that you could catch it from the dentist, or from an unsterilized acupuncturist's needle ... Did they get it because of their work?

—No, a crazy woman infected them five years ago ... They weren't the only ones: the two doctors in Bonvix and a surgeon from Niort who stayed in town were also infected, as well as a retired forest ranger ... They won't last much longer ...

A pickup artist in a grey suit with polished dress shoes, Ray-Bans glued to his face, and a husky on a leash greeted the vet enthusiastically, hoping for an invitation to join them. He had to settle for a brief nod, and disappeared toward the dock, towed by his sled dog.

—She would sleep with them, to give it to them?

—No ... She was a nurse ...

Gabriel kept up the questions, to see to what extent André Sloga's fiction was based on reality.

—How could someone pass on AIDS other than

by unprotected sex? Did they shoot up together without changing the needle? It's crazy, almost all of the doctors ...

The vet frowned.

—That's the rumor ... Each of them, for one reason or another, needed shots, and the nurse took the opportunity to fill the syringe with contaminated blood ...

—Unbelievable! She's been arrested, I hope ...

—The police didn't have to lift a finger: she was found murdered late one night in a stream, not two steps from here ... To this day nobody knows who killed her, no more than they know why she was so angry at the forest ranger and all the medical professionals of Bonvix.

—You must be very brave to take over!

—Not really ... I have two diplomas: veterinarian and nurse!

11

LUMINARIES AND LOUTS

The Parisian papers had fattened their headlines to announce a fresh pipe bomb attack in the streets of the capital city. This time, the anonymous terrorists had deposited their deadly parcel in a supermarket, in the meat aisle. As Gabriel was buying up a fistful of daily papers, his eyes were drawn to a local tabloid, the *Voice of the Marshes*, set on a shelf dedicated to the news of the region. The first page was almost entirely devoted to the resumption of the highway project that was mutilating a regional park, and below it were the election cards for the game of liar's poker that was playing out between Niort's socialist mayor and its socialist deputy, Ségolène Royal. A small box placed at the very bottom, to the right, which referred readers to the back pages, contained this bit of text: "The Return of the Audiat Affair: Valéric's Vengeance." He left the newsstand and walked a hundred or so meters along the riverbank until he got to one of four benches that had been installed beneath the plane trees surrounding the monument to Bonvix's dead. The full article comprised just a few hastily composed lines:

The Bonvix police recently received a visit from a man of about sixty whose identity is being withheld. This man, who apparently lives in the vicinity of Maillezais, gave the judicial authorities reliable information that may strongly influence investigations into a crime that put an end to a series of revenge-killings by the nurse Valérie Audiat, daughter of the eminent manufacturer Eugène Audiat. The examining magistrate, Pierre Tiercelet, is refusing to comment, recalling that the case was damaged early on by the effects of an overzealous haste to bring it to a close.

The piece was signed austerely by one "Fred. Lf.," whose full name, Fred Ledoeunf, Gabriel found deep in the paper's guts, on the second-to-last page.

In the center of the square, the bronze statue immortalizing victorious infantrymen pointed unwittingly, with an outstretched hand bearing a laurel branch, to the public toilets and telephone booth. Gabriel opened the shatterproof glass door and inserted his credit card into the slot. A sudden intuition made him dial the number of the hair salon. He didn't immediately recognize Cheryl from the distant "hello" that she reserved for clients making appointments. The usual warmth returned to her voice once she'd identified him.

—You could have called me earlier, I didn't sleep all night ... Where are you this time? Chechnya, East Timor, Rwanda?

—Even worse ... In the swamps of Poitiers!

He reassured her, promising to be back within a couple of days, and then dialed the number for the *Voice of the Marshes*.

An hour later he parked his Peugeot in the elevated lot in Fontenay-le-Comte, then took the pedestrian streets back into the historic district. The vaulted passageway the journalist had described opened up into a large interior courtyard paved with stone. The buildings around its perimeter were still recognizably those of an old farm: stables, grange, family home. A former barn was home to the offices of the *Voice of the Marshes*, and a meticulously restored sign reminded visitors that the paper, founded in 1868, had once been called *The Vendée Echo*.

Gabriel pushed open the glass-paned door that had been installed between two supporting posts and found himself in a vast, unpartitioned space into which a narrow glass transom cast a bit of diffused daylight. A worker was busy on an antique offset printer: running from the ink plates to the receiver, climbing onto the catwalk to give the rollers two or three turns by hand, continually adjusting the pressure of the grippers, the power of the suctions. The machine alone occupied three-quarters of the space; the piles of paper reams, pallets stacked with final editions, and disorganized heaps of back issues left only a tiny space for a newsroom, carved out of the most well-lit corner. Gabriel took advantage of a paper jam in the offset, caused by a sheet of paper falling prey to a sucker, to make his approach.

—May I see the editor in chief?

The printer gestured vaguely toward the piles. Gabriel circumnavigated the boxes of research; cases of film, ink, and photosensitive plates; sleeves and rubber blankets; and finally caught a glimpse of the journalist, who was, with one finger, pounding out an article on the keyboard of a new-model laptop set on an ancient marble shelf. He lifted a hand to make it clear that he knew someone was there but that he was in the midst of a crucial moment of composition. He coughed up a full paragraph before closing the computer and stretching out with a yawn. Gabriel took the time to observe him closely. Frédéric Ledoeunf looked like he had about sixty years and a hundred kilograms under his belt. The most immediately noticeable thing about him was the pair of enormous, thick glasses that sat as much on the bulge of his cheeks as on the tip of his nose; after that, it was the absence of his neck, which seemed to have been engulfed half by successive waves of his chin, and half by the mass of his shoulders.

—Are you Frédéric Ledoeunf?

—Since I was a boy, I've been trained by others to answer yes to that question.

He had a thin voice that contrasted comically with the voluminous form from which it emanated.

—Gabriel Lecouvreur. I telephoned about an hour ago ... About the nurse ...

He nodded.

—So you're interested in the Audiat affair? I thought everyone in Paris had tabled it. Which rag do you work for?

Gabriel came to sit on the edge of the sunlit table.

—I'm a private detective, not a journalist ...

The man's eyes lit up behind the cathedral glass protecting them.

—There's no need for such contrition! A private detective: it's the dream of every self-respecting journalist ...

You'll say there aren't many of *them* these days, okay, but the ones we have left are the very best! So, you've been hired to look into the Audiat affair?

—Not really ... I've hired myself ...

Ledoeunf contorted his mouth into an exaggerated frown that caused a good half of his double chin to disappear.

—That's not an auspicious starting point. I've never done the job myself, but I've read a lot about it, mostly in the Série Noir books ... You should probably stay away: in those stories, when a detective feels personally invested in a mission, usually nothing good happens to him ...

Gabriel liked the guy. He glanced at his watch.

—I try to survive on cigarettes and whisky, but I'm in the mood to cheat on my diet ... I saw an inn, just up the way from here ... How about we keep talking in front of a plate of your regional dishes?

—What's it called, this inn?

—I wasn't paying attention ... the terrace overlooks the Sèvre Niortaise ...

—Here, it's called the Vendée ... You may be clueless about geography, but you've got an eye for food and drink. That's an excellent spot ...

Ledoeunf took a minute to copy his text onto a diskette, which he gave to the offset operator before leaving the *Voice of the Marshes* printshop.

The well-appointed inn, with its tiled floor and exposed beams, was called, curiously, the Yes-But. In a short paragraph that appeared on the menus, the owner explained that the name had come to him after he'd repeatedly heard customers say, when asked if they wanted wine or a digestif: *Yes, but I'm driving.*

The journalist didn't need to look at the menu; he knew it by heart. They were served *eel au gratin* in dishes hot from the oven, accompanied by some Bonnezeaux, a white wine that doesn't travel well and is only drunk within a radius of fifty kilometers. Lost in a world of flavor, they ate in silence, their minds in their mouths. It was Ledoeunf who started the conversation up again, while using his fork to scrape the tiny crust of scorched cheese that had adhered to the inside of the dish.

—How about we show our hands right away? Do you have some kind of connection with the Audiat family, or with one of the people Valérie offed?

—No, I've been a Parisian since the beginning of time. My paternal ancestors from the iron age probably lived in a cave in Montmartre ... On my mother's side, it would have been a grotto in Belleville. This is the first time I've set foot in the marshes of Poitiers.

The journalist savored the last gulp of wine.

—By now we know almost everything about what made Valérie Audiat inject contaminated blood into the arteries of her lovers and clients ... We've established a fairly convincing hypothesis to explain how she herself was killed. This very evening, I wrote a detailed piece which should take up most of an upcoming edition of the *Voice of the Marshes.* Saturday's ...

Gabriel ordered a half-carafe of Bonnezeaux for the journalist and treated himself to a Tsingtao.

—Would it be possible for me to see it?

—I don't see any major inconvenience there. I would impose just two conditions ...

—Go ahead, I'll see if they're within my means.

—First, and even though I don't think anyone would take it, I'd want you to promise not to give the information to one of your journalist friends as soon as you leave here ...

—You are in a position to know that "friend" and "journalist" aren't words that go together very well ...

Ledoeunf acquiesced, batting his batrachian eyelashes.

—Noted. Second, I would like to be enlightened as to what brings you here, five years after the first-class cover-up of a considerable scandal, and three days before its denouement which, in my extreme pessimism, I suspect will be surrounded by the profoundest media silence ... To be completely frank, and it might be the alcohol talking now, I have to admit that I don't believe your story about being a self-employed detective for a minute! Are you independently wealthy?

Gabriel lifted his eyes to the sky and sighed.

—Strictly speaking, that is not far from the truth. I'm not rolling in it, but I manage to live comfortably from my job. If I wanted to show off, I could even tell you that I'm the owner of a small private plane that I keep at the Moisselles airport, but that would be unnecessary, wouldn't it?

—Life is like poker. You've got to play your hand . . . What kind of bird is it?

—A Polikarpov I-16 ...

Ledoeunf set down the glass of Cognac that he'd been warming in his hands.

—Seriously? The one Malraux writes about in *Man's Hope*?

—One and the same! You're one of the few people who remembers that ... I bought mine in Catalonia, a few years back ... The Soviets had sold it to the Spanish Republic in 1937, through France-Navigation, the Communist Internationale's maritime company, which acted as an intermediary. It was part of the Fourth Squadron, Mosca 31 ...

—Are you allowed to fly a fighter plane?

—Yes, once it's been disarmed ... For the moment, I'm restoring it, piece by piece. The reason I'm here is that someone whose work I love was badly beaten, just the day before yesterday, by some thugs, and I have every reason to believe that they wanted to prevent him from divulging what he'd learned about the Audiat affair ...

The journalist leaned back to drink his liqueur. The chair creaked beneath the force of his weight.

—What does your friend do? Is he also a private dick?

—No. He does what I've always dreamed of doing. He's a writer.

Ledoeunf nearly choked.

—Don't tell me you mean André Sloga!

—You know him too?

—What do you mean, do I know him! I know him better than anyone! We ate together at this very table three months ago ... I haven't seen anything about him being attacked. What happened?

Gabriel told him the little he knew about the attack on Rue Jeanne d'Arc, recounted his visits to the Pitié-Salpêtrière, and invented a plausible story to explain his acquaintance with *Moon over the Marshes*, the novelist's manuscript-in-progress. Ledoeunf listened to him attentively while indulging in a genuine cinnamon-scented Davidoff cigar.

—I don't want to discourage you, but I think you're on the wrong track. I don't see who would want to risk reviving the Audiat affair by attacking a Parisian writer ...

Gabriel interrupted him.

—But it's obvious: the murderer!

Ledoeunf sent a stream of Caribbean smoke up toward the ceiling.

—I can assure you that he is no longer capable of doing so!

—How can you be so sure?

—For the simple reason that he, too, is dead! The hand of justice has been dealt. That's the story I'm preparing for my paper.

Gabriel was stunned. The scenario he'd constructed while driving on the Aquitaine melted into nothing. If what the journalist was saying was true, then the trail of Valérie-Yolanda had ended abruptly, a red herring in a cul-de-sac. His dining companion planted his elbows on the table.

—This is a strange place, both endearing and repellent. When I arrived here in '73, still glowing from my brief stint at the crown jewel of the Parisian press—that's what they called *France-Soir* back then—my goal was to transform the old *Vendée Echo* into the *Vendée Fury*! I went public with some real scoops. That continued for two, three months ... Then in one fell swoop, every source went silent. I lost access to everything from the civil registry to the cafeteria menu!

Gabriel waved his credit card to call for the bill.

—And then?

—And then nothing ... I waited for it to pass, and then I joined the ranks ... I just needed to learn that around here, people will tell you anything as long as you assure them you won't use it ... It's the way the regional press works, but they don't explain that to you in journalism school: they take advantage of the naïveté of novices... The Audiat affair could easily be a case study for deciphering these invisible practices of censorship and self-censorship ... I didn't speak about it to André Sloga when he came to see me at the paper, but I'm thoroughly convinced that the police arrested that innocent vagrant, when the investigation had barely begun, for the sole reason of covering up the trail ... They had to put out the fire and offer a bogus story to the public so that everyone would be thinking the same thing!

—This would be plausible if it was your local celebrity Ségolène Royal who'd been found in the swamp ... But Valérie Audiat doesn't justify such a conspiracy of silence!

Ledoeunf let out a hiccup that made his shoulders shake.

—You're losing sight of the context. From the point of view of a Parisian, a man who is directly responsible for five hundred jobs, and indirectly for just as many, is nothing special. And it wouldn't mean anything that he is also the heir of one of the oldest families in the region. The fact that, in addition, he's vice president of the chamber of commerce, president of the Rotary club, and a councilman for the marshland's most important city, Bonvix, would only make him more of a rube in your eyes ... And yet, from the point of view of the people here, that's a considerable amount of power. Everyone is indebted to him for something: a job for their youngest child who's been acting out, help getting a loan from the Agricultural Credit Union, an intervention with a congressman or tax collector, a dispensation for a driver's license ...

—A powerhouse.

—Exactly. He can get anything done. And after we learned about the murder of his daughter, the entire region was walking on eggshells, starting with the cops. It was of the most urgent importance to disconnect this heinous crime from the family of the region's biggest benefactor. Hence the arrest of the wild coypu breeder ... Rumors had started to spread when the illness struck all of Bonvix's medical professionals, who shared the additional distinguishing feature of having been seen by Valérie: the pharmacist, the two doctors, the surgeon, and the vet, one after the other ...

—You've forgotten the forest ranger, the one Sloga called Fernand in his book ...

The journalist tapped his forehead with the tip of his index finger.

—Don't worry, I have the whole story here, perfectly intact! In reality, his name wasn't Fernand but Alfred Tourneur. He died first, from AIDS, less than a month after Valérie's murder. I knew her well as a child. Her father paraded her about like a mascot. Pretty as a picture, cunning as a fox; she conquered everything in her path. He talked about how he would make a scholar of her, how she'd be in line for a Nobel Prize, but at around seventeen, eighteen, things took a turn. She shut down and started to keep to herself, she let her studies go completely and settled for a shitty job as a nurse in the district run by her own father!

Gabriel felt a sense of fatigue descend on his shoulders. He had a vague idea about what Ledoeunf was going to throw at him, but he couldn't help asking the question.

—What had happened to her?

—The absolute worst horror ... For the daughter of a proletarian from Aubervilliers or for a wealthy Vandéean! She was raped after one of the debauched parties that are common here among the bourgeoisie. According to my sources, it took place in the gardens of the house belonging to Francois Corn, the surgeon from Niort ... The two doctors, the vet, and the pharmacist waited their turns ... The forest ranger approached when he heard Valérie's screams. She cried to him for help, but he did nothing, out of cowardice ... That was the night that changed her life, and every minute that followed was devoted to revenge ... She went off to study nursing, then came back to practice, settling back in as if nothing had happened, as if that horrible night never had occurred. Or so everyone thought ...

The eel rose up in Gabriel's throat; he downed the dregs of his Tsingtao in an effort to calm the nausea.

—And which one of the bastards killed her?

—None of them, in my view. Those men, now drowning in their own rotten blood, still don't know how the virus got to them ... They think they got unlucky with a one-night stand. It's even more terrible not knowing who to blame. No, the murderer is to be found elsewhere ... If you have five more minutes to spare, come to my office, and I'll show you his photo ...

12

WITH HIS TAIL BETWEEN HIS LEGS

When they pushed open the door to the printshop, the worker was finishing his bagged lunch, sitting on the ladder of the hulking press. Ledoeunf steered Gabriel toward a small furnished office in the back, behind the stockpiles of paper. He pulled out a large binder that contained a copy of every edition of the newspaper that had appeared since the beginning of the year, and shuffled through to find the one from the first week of July. He set it down on a ream bearing the Conquéror logo.

—That's him!

Gabriel leaned over the photo, which was framed with a thick black border and occupied most of the front page below the headline. You could sense the official nature of the posed shot, and how the figure facing the lens, a man of about sixty, was trying to present an image of himself as energetic, responsible. Gabriel read the blocky type that appeared above the portrait:

TRAGIC DISAPPEARANCE OF THE
INDUSTRIALIST EUGÈNE AUDIAT

He skimmed the opening of Ledoeunf's article, in which all

of the titular responsibilities of the President Director General Founder of the Society for Audiat's Metal Fabricators were enumerated. The important phrase was drowned in an accretion of commonplaces, a festival of fluff:

Monsieur Eugène Audiat never recovered from the murder of his daughter Valérie, on July 4, 1990, five years ago to the day. Those close to him connect that family tragedy with his own fatal act.

Ledoeunf closed the binder over the collection of newspapers.

—In my opinion, he killed his daughter when he found out what she'd done ... We'll never know the circumstances ... Anything is possible ... We can't even know whether he was aware of Valérie's own motive ...

Gabriel was visibly shaken.

—When André Sloga came to see you, in the spring, did you tell him what you just told me?

—Barely a tenth of it ... He didn't need me to: he'd been alert to the slightest shred of gossip for weeks. He knew almost everything already.

—All the more reason for someone wanting to shut him up ...

—In these parts, people settle scores the old-fashioned way. Why hire Parisian thugs when there was no lack of opportunities here in the swamps? It just wouldn't be done.

Gabriel walked over to the door. He turned back around when the printer started up the offset and the grippers began to claw at the void.

—You're going to put this in the next edition?

Ledoeunf lowered his eyes behind his bulletproof glasses. He pressed the palm of his hand to his head.

—The paper is here, in its ideal, perfectly calibrated state ... I don't think it's time yet to put it out ... I'm going to add two or three new bits of information, put an end to this whole Swamp Fever myth, and in a month, or at the most two, people will be ready to know the whole truth.

Gabriel could see from the look in the journalist's eyes that it would never happen, that the ideal paper would stay right where it was, nice and warm. Too much time had passed since Ledoeunf had abandoned his youth, his *Vendée Fury* ... The natives of Bonvix and its environs would learn more from buying Sloga's book, if he managed to finish it, than they would by subscribing to the *Voice of the Marshes* for ten years. Gabriel retrieved his car from the parking lot, near the arched bridge. The Vendée had turned grey, signaling the arrival of a storm. The first drops, fat and heavy, studded the windshield as Gabriel entered Bonvix. He settled up at the River Rat Inn and left, after first acquiring a cassette tape of Vendéen blues, the only local product he could find in the general store on the riverbank. He arrived in Paris under a downpour, accompanied by the accordion-backed strains of Jeaulin le Patoisant:

Wait for tomorrow, the world's end it will bring
My last will and testament's not finished yet
My ticket's reserved, my hands they are clean
Swept away right in front of my own doorstep

A riot of yellow-and-black signs, signaled by rows of blinking lights, had decommissioned two or three lanes of the autoroute, fifteen kilometers from the Porte de Saint-Cloud. Enormous highway maintenance vehicles clogged the parts of the road that had been freed of traffic. An army of workers in hardhats and boots poured out from the canvas-covered trucks, taking over the landscape. He struggled to follow the tortuous signage through the detour.

Cheryl was stuffing her daily half-meter-square of Parisian hair into a trashcan bearing the city's coat of arms when the Peugeot pulled up in front of the Kurdish restaurant that had just opened across from the salon. She kissed him without uttering the slightest reproach for his escapade. As soon as they'd entered the apartment, she started in on the carcass of a roasted chicken, picking it over for hidden remnants of flesh, and lined up an impressive number of jarred herbs and spices on the kitchen counter.

—What are you making us?

—Poet's rice ...

He understood that this would be his only punishment.

—Poet's rice? What do you put in that, feet?

—That's the best you can do? It's supposed to be very good. A customer gave me the recipe. You've seen her ... Zaraounia, the sister of the Mauritian filmmaker. I do her hair every other week ...

—Hair-shmair! That still doesn't tell me what I'm going to find on my plate ...

Cheryl shrugged and browned two cups of basmati rice in some olive oil. When the grains had turned translucent, she doused them in six parts water and added a spiced bouillon cube. She added three shakes each from the jars of rosemary, fines herbes, ground garlic, basil, parsley, and herbes de Provence into the casserole dish. She stirred them in with a wooden spoon, then added a good dose of mild curry, which gave the mixture some color. On the other burner, she was slowly browning the onions along with the scraps of chicken meat, which she tossed in with the rice once nearly all the water had evaporated. Gabriel sampled his first forkful of poet's rice. Cheryl watched him, vaguely apprehensive.

—So, how is it?

He was surprised to hear himself respond:

—Excellent ... When you see how it's made, you fear the worst ... It could use some salt, but that's all ...

They went to bed early, and Cheryl, whose turn it was, established the rules of the game for the night.

—No hands!

13

DISKS, CHICKS, AND TRICKS

The next morning, Gabriel lounged around in bed until almost eleven, poring over bits of André Sloga's manuscript, looking for a hidden meaning. Thanks to Ledoeunf's prodigious descriptions, he was able to put a real name to each character portrayed by the novelist, but he discovered nothing that would help advance his investigation into the swampy murder.

He took a bath in the circular tub that Cheryl had had made to her specifications and installed in the heart of her exquisite apartment. A former graffiti artist turned interior decorator had reproduced a winter landscape by Breugel the Younger on the wall, replacing all the men with the mistress of the house's favorite animal: the kangaroo.

Gabriel piled his dirty clothes in the wicker hamper, threw on a pair of jeans and a shirt, and planted himself at the living room table. All the things he'd collected having to do with André Sloga were gathered on the tablecloth, which bore the image of Marilyn Monroe: the manuscript, the receipt from Docutec, the package from the bookseller and the letter from the royalties company, the anonymous note, the book by Joseph Délteil, and the transcription of the author's words from the Pitié: "Max, the loudspeaker, on the square." He racked his brain fruitlessly, trying out new groupings, new juxtapositions. When the clock struck noon at Saint-Ambroise de Popincourt, he decided to give up. Just then, as he was putting everything back into one of the plastic bags he used in lieu of a filing cabinet, the diskette from Docutec fell onto the pink carpet. He picked it up, then waved it in front of his face like a fan before finally sliding it into its paper sleeve.

The Atlantic storms that were predicted in all the reports hadn't yet come to disperse the pollution from the Parisian streets, and Maria was helping Vlad set up tables on the sidewalk of Avenue Ledru-Rollin for customers with a penchant for exhaust. Inside, all the tables were taken. Gabriel hoisted himself onto a bar stool next to an African man absorbed in the financial pages of *Libération*. Gérard presented him with a Kriek Lambic from Ventoux that the sales rep from Kabyle Distributors had dug up for him.

—Try this! Still not as good as Bécasse, but it's not far off. In two or three years at the most, if they don't slack off, these brewers from Carpentras'll be giving the Belgians a run for their money! You want to eat something? The Special of the Day is pigs' feet ...

—That's not the Special of the Day, that's the Special of Every Day!

—You're the only one complaining. I'm on two best-of lists this year ...

—You're getting gullible! Makes me want to ... All right, bring me your feet ...

Gabriel gorged himself on rind and gelatin, and as was his custom, left nothing but a necklace of ossicles around the edge of his plate. Old Léon came over to rub up against him. He sniffed at his dog food, didn't taste it, and retreated to the back of the restaurant, plowing into anyone who stood in his way. Gabriel took out the diskette and showed it to Gérard, who was working the percolator.

—What kind of computer do you have?

—An old Mac Classic ...

—Can I go upstairs and see what happens if I put in this diskette?

The African man lifted his head from his valuations and laughed. Gabriel laughed back.

—Did I say something funny?

—You said "diskette" ...

The detective frowned.

—And when someone says "diskette," that makes you laugh?

—Especially when you say that you're going to "put it in" ... In Sénégal, where I'm from, a diskette isn't that plastic square. A diskette is what you'd call a slut in Dakar ... An attractive girl who's easy to get ...

Gérard, beaming, pointed upstairs.

—Well then, listen to the man: Take your diskette upstairs and put it in; it'll help you digest!

The apartment above the Sainte-Scolasse was like a miniature version of one of the greenhouses in the Jardin des Plantes. Summer and winter, Maria kept it at a constant 24 degrees Centigrade and 66 percent humidity, with the exception of the kitchen and the bedroom. The walls were hidden behind clumps of *evaniscus*, *rogrindas*, rose laurels. A Virginia creeper had taken over the arbor on the balcony,

Mexican *bifithéums* luxuriated in the bathtub, hops plants with mauve flowers clung to the curtain rods ... The old-style Mac sat imposingly on a shelf, next to the conjugal bed. Gabriel turned it on and the opening notes of "En rouge et noir" by Jeanne Mas welcomed him to the land of Apple. He inserted the diskette and an icon appeared near the upper-right edge of the screen. He clicked on it to open the folder. Four icons appeared:

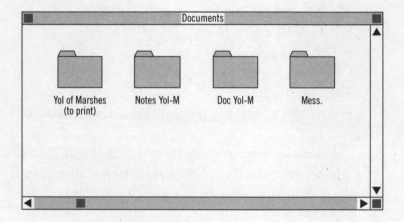

Gabriel skimmed through the first file, which turned out to be identical to the manuscript given to him by the salesgirl-in-training at Docutec; the second folder contained summaries of conversations between Sloga and the main players in the Audiat affair; and in the third was an inventory of everything that had been written on the subject since the discovery of Valérie-Yolanda's corpse. He read it all in detail without learning anything he didn't already know. Deflated, he clicked on the last icon: *The Mess*. After reading nothing but the title and subtitle, he understood that he'd just been given a substantial lead:

DANGEROUS LIAISONS

Fifty years later, the messengers of hate return.

The ten pages didn't include a single name. It was a frightening collage of quotations that had been painstakingly dated and footnoted. Gabriel took a look at the opening excerpt.

JEWISH COWARDICE IN
THE PRESIDENTIAL PALACE

The Jews of P.S. are eaten away on the inside thanks to cronyism at the end of Mitterand's reign.

The cowards. They had believed that his meeting with Arafat was just another one of the pathetic little parentheses they were going to have to get used to, given their patron's advancing age. So they painfully held their tongues. Well, the yellow Jews in the government never say anything. To be Jewish in the P.S. during these years of compliance, of European turbulence and Euro-Arab dialogue, isn't simple. Attali is a major Jewish writer; in his most recent novel he cites the Book of Creation and mixes Hebrew esotericism with a straightforward narrative, but still, his identity as an intellectual has not seemed to inspire him to rectify—not even for the sake of his image as a Hassid—Mitterand's empty words.

Of course it's the same with Stirn, Fabius, and the others (Lang!) too.

Continental Fury, No. 26, 8 November 1989

Gabriel quickly skimmed a dozen nauseating passages from *Our Friends the Singers*, volumes one and two, only to get stuck on the first lines of an article about Patrick Bruel in which it was revealed that the man with the "broken voice" was born Maurice Benguigui; this permitted the author to refer to him from then on as the singer with three "i"s: one for Patrick, two for Benguigui. Gabriel remembered how Le Pen had taken advantage of the revelation.

The third bit of filth originated from the June 1979 edition of the *Social War*, and was somberly titled *Who Are the Jews?*:

The legend of the "gas chambers" was legitimized at the Nuremberg Trials, when the Nazis were judged by their vanquishers. Its primary function was to enable the Stalino-Democrats to distinguish themselves absolutely from the Nazis and their allies. Antifascism and Anti-Nazism have allowed them to justify their own acts of war, and continue to justify many ignominies since then.

But the real ignominies reached a new level with a passage from the *Paris Imbecile*, No. 5, from December 1991:

By replacing the celebration of the *Übermensch* (the super-human) with that of the *Untermensch* (the sub-human), by taking the handicapped instead of the Aryans as a model for man's future, by insisting on a degrading survival rather than a pragmatic elimination, by replacing the "final solution" with a procreative ideology, we are producing markedly analogous results: a Hell of congenital cripples condemned to live, forced therapies and torture for the dying, the overpopulation of the third world—in other words, famine and genocide.

Gabriel closed the icon and sent the entire "Mess" folder to print. The taste of bile filled his mouth. He grabbed the closest bottle from the bar beneath the television and swallowed a long pull of wine, both bitter and sweet, which he spit back up when he realized it was of the fortified kind. The printer chanted some notes from "En rouge et noir" to signal that it had completed its mission. He set the printed pages on the edge of the shelf, reading only a few lines at the bottom, from the weekly *Minute-France*, No. 1695, November 4, 1992:

... Laurent Fabius is monstrous, I mean, worthy of exhibition. As an infant, swaddled by provincial nannies to whom his leftist parents barely spoke,

Laurent never learned the dialect of "pi-pi, ka-ka, do-do" that pediatricians call Picado. Laurent never said "ga-ga." The first word clearly formulated by the baby was "dollars!" Dead end of the Left, with his deadened maw, gelatinous jay ...

He remembered one of André Sloga's books that nobody had wanted after the war, a book that was then put out by an economically suicidal publisher, Paul Draflos, at the height of the leftist wave of the 1970s. The novel was called *The Handover* and recounted the story of a resistance movement from the Pyrenees, made up primarily of Spanish republicans who had refused to pick up arms again in 1944. These were men who planned to try the magistrates and cops who had aided and abetted the Nazis. They also thought that no victory would be complete without the fall of the Iberian dictators, Franco and Salazar. In the end, their romantic dream had drowned in blood at the hands of the united forces of France's new legitimacy.

Gabriel knew that Sloga, after his participation in the International Brigades, had joined the resistance again in Yonne. He could well imagine his reticence to aim his Sten at leaders who had become "reasonable."

It was clear, in any case, that fifty years later he'd rejoined the resistance.

With a Mac loaded to the gills with diskettes!

14

PEDRO AND THE NAZIS OF THE LEFT

Pedro Ferrer lived on the Quai Sisley in Villeneuve-la-Garenne, in an old barge that had been towed to within a hundred meters of the riverbank, just next to the Van Praët naval yards. The steel hull was burrowed into the black earth of the Paris Basin, and through its portholes the mysteries of vegetal life—various roots, worms, and insects—could be observed. Little by little, Pedro had added rooms to both sides of the boat, so that a first-time visitor would be surprised, after entering the maze of crudely constructed annexes, to emerge into the oblong enormity of the hold. It was there that he had set up his shop for stamping and engraving. In the era of decolonization and national liberation, this was where false papers, dozens at a time, were made to look official. More recently—the qualifier having taken precedence over the noun, with "national" everywhere supplanting "liberation"—the pace had significantly slowed. He'd become wary, working only through two or three intermediaries who were also trusted friends. Gabriel was one of them.

—What mischief are you up to now?

Pedro waved the flame of his lighter in front of the uneven stub of his Boyard Maïs and took a long puff. He could pride himself on being the last person in the world to smoke this brand of cigarette. When, several years earlier, the Surgeon General had decided to halt the fabrication of the most deadly of the human-lung-seeking missiles, Pedro had hastened to order a pallet full, which he stored in a damp and airless room near the propeller head. By his calculations, at a rate of twelve a day, he had enough to last him until his seventieth birthday, in the year 2000. He placed a blank sheet atop the disorderly stack of papers on the table.

—Just some BS so I don't lose my touch ...

—If it's BS, why are you hiding it? Don't you trust me anymore?

Pedro slapped him lightly on the back.

—This isn't true for everything, but in this particular case, the less you know the better ... What brings you here?

Gabriel explained what had happened to Sloga and why, after his time with the coypus of Poitiers, he was losing faith in his original hypothesis, seductive as it was, about vengeance over a literary indiscretion. Now he believed the attack on the writer might be related to his research into the revival of an openly fascist movement among Parisian intellectuals.

—I took the time to read and reread the veritable dictionary of putrid ideas that André Sloga had assembled from more than a hundred citations. It's revolting. He drew up charts in order to classify them according to their principal themes. Anti-Semitism and revisionism came first, followed close behind by a visceral hatred of social democracy, then by the denunciation of Satanic America, and finally, the celebration of nationalism in all its forms. The texts were taken from about thirty different publications. *Continental Furor* and the *Shock of the Month*, monthlies catering to intellectuals in the National Front, provided the majority of the references, but others were drawn from the *National Weekly*, the *Minute, Elements, Krisis, Humanity*, the *Social War*, the *People's Struggle, Revolution*, and a privately circulated bulletin of the Federation of Anarchists.

Pedro registered what he was being told. He sat down in an armchair that resembled Sylvia Krystel's in *Emmanuelle*, with the slight difference that this one was positioned beneath a portrait of Puig Antich, one of the last of Franco's victims. He read calmly for an hour, through his half-moon glasses, then put down the dozen or so sheets of paper with a disgusted frown. Gabriel sat down across from him.

—What do you think?

—Not much ... I get the sense that history is repeating itself, and that these cretins are serving stale dishes from the 1930s! That thing about Fabius, for example, that your friend found in the *Minute*, the Jewish baby who thinks only of dollars, that's vintage Léon Daudet ... The guy who wrote that isn't treading any new ground, I'm sure he stole "deadened maw, gelatinous jay" directly from old pamphlets by that Nazi piece of crap!

—What I like about you is that you don't bother with niceties, or subtle turns of phrase ...

Pedro's fist slammed down on the table, making his forger's tools jump.

—Because you think the way to hunt a hyena is with a flute! I give as much of a shit about political correctness as I do about being arrested! No mercy for the Krauts ... They must be crushed to the last. And not in the name of truth or reason! It's the fundamental, ancient instinct to survive. They proved what they're capable of, and if we let them sit at the table, they won't settle for just one seat.

Gabriel smiled as he listened to the diatribe.

—Seems like that did you good! You look revived. I've known for a long time what your convictions are, Pedro, but right now what I need is an objective, clear opinion about this steaming pile of manure.

Pedro relit his Boyard.

—If you hadn't forgotten how to be a student, you'd notice that I've already responded in part ... Did I or did I not tell you that they're just serving cold dishes from the '30s?

Gabriel knitted his brow.

—Yes. And?

—And how the hell does this happen? We teach kids the color of the uniforms Francois I's soldiers wore when they raided Marignan in 1515, but they are incapable of learning what happened just thirty years before they were born! What really alarms me in this collage of quotations is the conflation of ideas from right-wing and communist presses. You know me well enough to know that I puke on all manner of commies, whether they're Stalinists, Trotsky-ites, Marxists, Leninists, Carilloists, Maoists, Guevaroists, or Jivaroists! And yet, Kronstadt, Makhno, and the Catalogne won't let me forget that we're all fuel for the fascists' fire ... Because we're Jewish, Arab, black, anarchist, handicapped, queer, or all of the above, like you!

—I was waiting for that, you couldn't resist ...

—It might be a cheap shot, but it gives me joy ...

Seriously, there's nothing more dangerous than an alliance between the fascists and the commies ... It's like nitrite and glycerine. In two separate bottles you've got nothing to fear, but if you mix them, you'll blow your head off! The Number Two in the French Communist Party, Jacques Doriot, deputy mayor of Saint-Denis, crossed over at the end of the 1930s, but luckily his party threw him out. He died wearing an S.S. uniform. Imagine the scene if he'd gotten away with it, if he'd taken down Thorez ... It was a close call ...

Gabriel picked up an awl and started cleaning his fingernails.

—We aren't at that point yet ...

Pedro took the tool from him.

—Go tell that to the flock in Toulon, Orange, Marignane, Dreux, Clichy-sous-Bois ... Le Pen's horde has become the number one labor party in France! It's all but taken the lead even in Drancy, the city where an old Socialist, Laval, deported seventy thousand Jews in a raid carried out by our beloved forces from the Order! I shit upon every mute Drancean with his memory up his ass!

Pedro rose suddenly, causing the wicker to creak, and went over to the library that had been built into what was formerly the bargeman's sleeping alcove.

—Here, I know exactly what all this shit you've shown me has made me think of! It must be in the section for ... Hold on ... You can judge for yourself ...

His hand caressed the edges of a row of books and pamphlets. He delicately extracted a booklet with a brown cover, whose yellowed pages were separating from the spine, and blew on it to disperse the dust. Gabriel was only able to read the title, *Black Front*, before Pedro set it on the table and opened to the flyleaf, which bore an epigraph from Adolf Hitler:

"There are more things that link us to communism than things that separate us. There is, above all, the revolutionary spirit. The social democrat and the bourgeois unionist will never become National Socialists, but the communist will."

Gabriel read the text several times.

—For fuck's sake. He's never been one of my favorite authors, far from it, but I didn't suspect he was capable of such reflection ... People talk about him like he was a born imbecile.

Pedro flipped through the little book, and entire passages returned to him from memory. It was enough to replace the 1930s with the 1990s to see how much the strategy of an alliance between red and brown persisted. He looked at Gabriel.

—So many things have been swept under the carpet ... Have you heard about the Strasser brothers, the left-wing Nazis?

—No, and even the concept of a left-wing Nazi is new to me, I must admit!

—Well, there are two brothers, Otto and Gregor, who, in around 1925, start to establish the Nazi party in northern Germany, in the provinces of Prussia, Saxony, Rhineland, and Hanover ... These aren't little guys ... Their right-hand man is a guy called Goebbels. Gregor Strasser quickly becomes Number Two in the Nazi party, and the leader of Hitler's deputies in the Reichstag. He tries to set up an anti-capitalist program: confiscation of property from the old reigning families, nationalization of heavy industry and of the banks, expropriation of holdings. He allies himself with the red unions, the tramways and metalworkers, and even threatens Hitler with exclusion ... In 1934, after his party comes into power, he attempts a rapprochement with the three million men of Ernst Röhm's assault division ... His former right-hand man, who has gone back to Hitler's side, has them all executed in June of that year, during the Night of the Long Knives. Otto Strasser escapes, with the killers in pursuit. He hides away in Austria, in Chechnya, in Canada. He made a comeback in Berlin in the early 1970s, creating a new national Bolshevik party, the German Social Union. But he arrived too early: it was a flop. Today, he'd have a good chance of succeeding.

Pedro held out the pamphlet to Gabriel.

—Shall I leave it with you?

—Thanks, I'll read it tonight while watching *Where Are They Now?*

—I don't see the connection ...

—Neither do I!

15

THE RUSSIAN POET WHO
LOVES SERBIAN SHRINKS

The storm broke just as Gabriel passed the prow of the barge, on which you could still read the name *Carmela*. He pushed open the makeshift door to Pedro's vegetable garden. The Seine instantly turned the same shade of grey as the department-store warehouses that lined the horizon. The raindrops, like those he'd wiped away on his return from Bonvix, burst on the hard earth, and flashes of lightning split the dark sky into pieces above the Île-Saint-Denis. Gabriel pulled his jacket up over his head and ran all the way to the Peugeot, which was parked in front of the closed shutters of the Guinguette des Chantiers. In the notebook that sat on top of the glove box, he'd written down the addresses, telephone and fax numbers of all the publishers in André Sloga's inventory. He noticed that one of the most cited papers, *Continental Furor*, had long shared a Gennevilliers address with the offices of Éditions Gaston Lémoine. He crossed both branches of the river and followed its meanderings to the square surrounding the city hall, which had been afflicted with a polychromatic fountain by one of the numerous lumpish students of Fernand Léger.

Éditions Lémoine's headquarters were tucked away in

an industrial zone occupying the wastelands that bordered the A86. Pallets of printed matter cinched with plastic bands waited in the parking lot to be loaded into a semi. Gabriel leaned over the freshly inked sheets. A four-color cover of *The History of the Militia,* printed eight to the sheet, awaited transportation to the bindery. The illustration referenced the poster from the young fascist movement's first congress: a fist holding a sword, raised up against a background of fields and factories and a red and black sky. He was astonished to notice that the group's logo was virtually identical to the red ribbon of the anti-AIDS campaigns. He had begun to read the text on the back cover when a voice made him jump.

—Are you looking for something?

He turned to face a paunchy skinhead of about thirty, decked out in cargo pants, camo shirt, and khaki Doc Martens. His hands were stained with ink. Gabriel pointed to the warehouse.

—Is the office in there?

—No, these are the studios … You have to go around …

Before moving away, the detective put his hand on the pile of book covers.

—Can't wait for this to be out in the stores! They fill our heads with so much junk, we're in danger of forgetting to learn from their example …

A toothy smile spread across the skinhead's pudgy face.

At first sight, the lobby of the Éditions Gaston Lémoine resembled the lobby of any business: impersonal decoration, all-purpose furnishings, insufficient lighting, the scent of photocopies. If, while reclining in one of the faux-leather armchairs, you felt the urge to read one of the magazines piled up on a Chinoiserie side table, you'd look in vain for the usual fare: *Paris-Match, Marie-Claire,* or the day's *Le Figaro.* On the other hand, if you were a lover of the exploits of various army corps—German, Japanese, Croatian, or Romanian, between 1939 and 1944—you'd be in heaven. It was clear to Gabriel that the clients of this establishment all belonged to the latter category. He flipped through a copy of *New Solidarity,* the main media outlet of the European Workers' Party, in which one of the directors of Éditions Gaston Lémoine—a certain Victor Brignard—made clear in a long interview that he was a member of that small, anti-Semitic group. He looked up. The receptionist had been trying for some time to replace the paper roll in the fax machine by putting it in backwards. Gabriel went behind the desk to assist her. The machine blinked in satisfaction.

—Thank you, I thought I'd never manage. Do you have an appointment?

—No, but I would like to see Monsieur Gaston Lémoine ...

—I'm afraid that will be difficult to arrange: he's been dead for half a century ... If you tell me what brings you here, I may be able to direct you ...

Gabriel lowered his voice.

—It's rather confidential ...

Her expression was as hypocritical as that of a mother leading her child to the dentist's chair.

—I assure you, it's no accident that I'm sitting at this desk ... I work closely with the director, Monsieur Brignard. Every file passes through my hands ... I know everything that goes on here.

Gabriel pretended to gather his courage.

—All right ... After the recent death of my father, I inherited a lot of family papers. Photo albums, collections of postcards, packets of letters ...

He noticed that she was showing signs of impatience.

—There were also a lot of documents from the period of the Occupation ... Files that had been examined by my grandfather, notebooks filled with intelligence never before seen ... All I've done so far is try to put them in some kind of order, but I think there is enough material to make an explosive book ...

He now had the full attention of Brignard's deputy.

—What kinds of files, what kinds of intelligence? Relating to what region?

—My grandfather was the archivist of the Rhône prefecture, in Lyon, and from what I've been able to understand, he kept copies of all the internal documents concerning the Militia and the Franc-Garde ...

She asked him to follow her to the second floor and handed him off to a short man with beady eyes who introduced himself as the literary director of Éditions Gaston Lémoine. Gabriel continued to play the role of the dutiful grandson carrying out a family obligation. He promised to return the next day with some samples from the Lyon documents. Before letting him leave, the beady-eyed man asked how he'd become aware of his enterprise and the ideological war it was waging.

—I subscribed to *Continental Furor* for many years, and I was always aware that it was printed here ...

Reassured, and eager to cement his hold on the heir, the beady-eyed man turned confessional.

—Our role wasn't limited to that ...

—It's too bad it's disappeared ...

—Yes. We owned nearly fifty percent of the paper. Forty-eight percent, to be precise. Our director, Victor Brignard, had even taken over its editorship for several years ... We could have done great things if the founder of the *Continental Furor*, Kevin Kervan, hadn't suddenly gone mad, blinded himself ... It never pays to cut corners ...

The beady-eyed man left him in the second-floor hallway, near the stairway. Gabriel descended it slowly, with one eye on the publications exhibited in small, glassed-in nooks. It wasn't pornography, but it was thoroughly obscene: Hitlerian, Mussolinian, Pétainian. Nothing here belonged in the hands of citizens between the ages of seven and seventy-seven. He froze at the top of the last flight of stairs when he heard the receptionist whispering into the telephone.

—You ask Roger to fill in for you. No ... Listen, Francis, you'll do what I say, ok? We need to find out more about this guy. If there's no other way, bring him to your meeting ... The boss wants to know what to expect from these archives ... We can't let this pass us by ... Understood? Don't slip up. Find a way.

Gabriel waited for a long moment on the landing before descending briskly, with a casual air. The receptionist flashed him a broad smile that lasted through his "See you tomorrow." The skinhead was in the parking lot, laboring over an all-terrain motorcycle that was apparently refusing to start. He lowered the kickstand and walked over to Gabriel, who was opening the door to the Peugeot.

Excuse me, but my bike won't start ... Are you driving to Paris?

—Yes ...

—Do you think you might be able to drop me off at the Porte d'Asnières? It's on the way ...

In order to sit down, he had to move André Sloga's papers to the backseat. Two sheets slipped out. While gathering them from the floor, the skinhead caught a few choice phrases from the *Continental Furor* concerning Bernard-Henri Lévy, which bolstered his trust in his accidental chauffeur:

> Bernard-Henri Lévy, the almost-philosopher who is not a writer, in a fat book published by Grasset ...
> Too much rigor annoys B.H.L., who has seen nothing, written nothing, made nothing, except cash, and always with the help of others ...

> B.H.L., a sad character whom I will finish off one day with a Moulinex kitchen knife ...

To see Lévy's name paired with the words "fat" and "cash" and the avowal of a murderous impulse: he was in familiar territory. The car crossed over the ring road and wove through the housing projects. Beyond small talk, the skinhead printer had a hard time formulating questions, keeping up a conversation. Rhetoric was not his strong point. Gabriel did not push him, and they continued on in silence.

He turned toward him after stopping at a red light, a hundred meters from the corner of Boulevard Berthier.

—Shall I leave you here or at the metro?

—This is good ... Nice of you to drop me off. But if you have a little time, I could offer you a drink, around here ...

—I won't say no.

The Saussure served only ordinary beers, and the foam on the Adelscott on tap that Gabriel ordered disintegrated as soon as it touched his lips, leaving behind two craters that resembled eyes floating in a soup. Francis lit up a Celtique and drank his Pelforth straight from the bottle, like a man.

—Would I be wrong to say that I have a feeling we're interested in some of the same things ...

Gabriel played the innocent.

—That would depend on what you're alluding to.

Francis looked around him. He leaned forward and whispered.

—Real History, the end of the lie spread by the lobby of ...

Gabriel considered the difficulty of his task. He had just entered into contact with his first fascists, and it was already impossible for him to rise to the challenge of having a simple conversation. He tried a new tack, tapping the skinhead's shoulder in a friendly way. They toasted, glass to bottle.

—Tonight, I'm on duty at a meeting just around the corner from here ... It's closed, but if you show up with me, there won't be a problem ... It's in honor of one of ours who's returned from Serbia ... He fought with the Dragan militias, in Krajina ...

—I didn't know Frenchmen could be admitted to the ranks of … Serbian nationalists …

Francis flashed a proud smile as if to say, "You don't know who you're talking to, my friend!"

—There are quite a few of our comrades there, but tonight it's a Russian who will take the stage: Ivan Astrapov.

Gabriel started when he heard the name. A dozen years ago he had demonstrated in support of political exile for a Soviet painter named Astrapov, who had been persecuted by Brezhnev's administration. His paintings weren't interesting in the least, but he had seemed to be a talented dissident. Gabriel pushed away his glass.

—Astrapov? Is he related to the painter?

—Same guy. But now he only paints with a gun! Preferably a machine gun.

16

IN THE FIELD

Gabriel let him pay for the drinks before following him along Boulevard Berthier. Young but battle-weary women, their arms perforated like colanders, sat on the trunks of parked cars and opened their thighs to the passing truck drivers. They passed by the old general stores that had been converted into scenery lots for the Opera de Paris and took a back alley that went along the tracks of the Saint-Lazare line.

Francis nodded to a guy who seemed to be busily tying his bootlace, and they were given the green light to go in. They entered the courtyard of an old warehouse. Another man was waiting on the loading dock. He took hold of Francis's wrist for a Roman handshake, and after consulting with him about Gabriel, he led them into a freight elevator, closed the heavy grille on them, and flipped the worn switch that hung from a wire. The elevator began to tremble violently, rising in fits and starts to the second level. Nearly two hundred people, the vast majority of them young men, were gathered in the former warehouse, whose walls and beams retained the pronounced odor of the coffee that had been packaged there for decades. Two young men who could have been Francis's twin brothers brought drinks to tables amidst the din of conversation. The sounds of the Serbian rock group Junak spilled from the PA, drowning out everything else. The skinhead printer sat Gabriel near the remains of a pulley system, and took up his post to the left of the entrance. A meter-high platform supported a table equipped with microphones and three chairs. The wall was decorated with multiple Serbian flags, spotted with stains and dust. They framed an enlarged photo of a Chechnyan squadron in traditional battle dress, with high black boots, thick beards, and fur hats.

Gabriel ordered a Tsver, brewed in Moscow according to the label. He drank it in small sips while observing the audience, which was composed for the most part of minor hoodlums from good families come out for their monthly thrill, and local dropouts looking for any kind of adventure to help them escape the endless void of their futures. At first he didn't recognize a single face: the small anonymous crowd of meetings ... But then, as he turned around to inspect the tables in the back, his gaze stopped on a man of about forty. It took him a good quarter of an hour to wrest the memory from his head and superimpose it onto the wide, ruddy face, prominent cheekbones, and unruly hair of Thierry Tegret. He'd met him two or three times during his first year at university. At that time, Thierry was the Number Two of a small, very active Trotskyist group, organized like an army. He commanded thirty or so militants who would march out of class on command. Gabriel had heard him talked about, vaguely, ten years later, when his organization denounced him publicly, accusing him of having embezzled funds of unknown origin. Here, he was flanked by a former reporter for the leftist paper *Libération*, Paul Estèphe, a specialist in the kind of shady business dealings that trade in the moods of the Cabinet Minister's staff, the stench of favoritism, the musk of bedrooms. Gabriel could still remember some of his appearances on the trashy shows on TeleFrance 1, where he talked about the gay pastor Joseph Doucé or the suicide of Pierre Bérégovoy. Thierry Tegret got up, and Gabriel thought that he was coming straight over to him. But the ex-militant for the extreme left passed him by to throw himself into the arms of a short-statured man with eyes hidden behind smoky wraparound glasses. Tegret hoisted himself onto the stage and extended his hand to the stocky masked man. A third man followed suit, and they sat down at the table. The silence was immediate. Tegret tapped on the microphones to check the sound, then began to speak.

—Dear comrades. I believe it's time to move on to the most important part of tonight's meeting. I would like to introduce to you, first, Commander Jovan Gavrovic, whose troops have valiantly resisted the Croato-Muslim coalition in the region of Bihac.

He paused for a burst of applause. Gavrovic, who did not speak a word of French, thanked everyone in Serbian and the applause redoubled.

—I don't need to waste my breath telling you about our brother Ivan Astrapov, who just spent three months on various European fronts where the continuity of our civilization is being threatened by the expansion of Muslim integrationism. In Chechnya, in Serbia! I only need to remind you, before asking Ivan Astrapov a series of questions, that I am here tonight in my capacity as editor in chief of *Nation First*, the daily paper for French social issues, in which Ivan will be publishing his combatant's notebook.

The atmosphere was stifling. Gabriel edged back toward the entrance, where a light current of air drifted in.

—My first question will be direct, dear Ivan. A film on the BBC showed you in the process of shooting up Sarajevo. Some claimed it was just for the cameras ...

The ex-Soviet ex-dissident ex-painter lowered the microphone to his mouth and pushed his glasses up onto the bridge of his nose. He had almost no accent, as is the case with people who've been to the best schools.

—If they stand in front of me, they'll have their answer! Tegret cheered along with the crowd.

—Do you think you killed one or many Bosnians?

—Over there, they're called Turks! I certainly hope I didn't waste any bullets ...

Francis passed in front of Gabriel, who forced a smile. On stage, the interview continued.

—What does it feel like as a painter to trade a paintbrush for a Kalashnikov?

—One hour of war, and you're forever cured of painting, of the illusion that it's possible to represent the world, to interpret it! What a waste of time! You have to smash it! Assault it, take it back! The reality of shooting at your sworn enemies gives you a sensation of strength, of freedom ... It's an immense joy. I've fought in Moldavia, in Slovenia, in Bosnia, in Abkhazia, in Krajina, and everywhere I've felt the same intense pleasure ... I have never felt as free as when I'm surrounded by the burning houses of Muslims, the stench of

Turkish corpses, the odor of cowards' piss! Art can't hold its own against that …

A religious silence accompanied these words, which he delivered with impassive eyes behind his corrective lenses.

—In your opinion, will these wars remain limited to the old grounds of the former Soviet empire?

Astrapov took a breath.

—If you want to know my real opinion, I would like for the Russian nationalists to get over the liberal illusion of their alcoholic czar and his prime minister, Pileofshitski, who has destroyed our race, our people! It's time to go on the offensive. If we act now, things could be settled quickly, with a minimum of damage. If we wait, we're looking at deaths by the thousands.

Tegret sensed that the audience had become very attentive, receptive.

—The liberal illusion is another name for democracy … Does that word make you afraid? Does it disgust you?

Astrapov stood up and leaned toward the room, shouting now:

—What about you, what do YOU think about democracy?!

A wall of boos rose to meet him. He sat back down, his face red.

—I could give a fuck about the Parisian democracies of Fabius, Lang, Stirn, and Stasi like I give a fuck about the New York democracies of Rockefeller and Metro-Goldwyn-Mayer! May they peacefully rot and die in their respective holes. I am simply asking the question: How long will we tolerate wars waged exclusively on the poor?

The audience stood in a single motion and chanted Astrapov's name. Only Commander Jovan Gavrovic, with whom no one could communicate, was left with his ass glued to his chair. Gabriel took advantage of the warriors' communion to slip away. The freight elevator was more efficient and quieter going down. It deposited him in front of the skinhead on duty, who quickly concealed his pistol, while checking tenderly to make certain it was loaded.

17

THE END OF THE WORLD

Gabriel had neither the strength nor the lack of judgment to go home. Better to go for a spin first. He took the Peugeot out to the interior ring road and drove, keeping the speedometer at a constant 140 KPH. The radar sensors flashed twice on his circular flight. Of the exits spelled out on the blue overpass signs, none was the one he needed. He spun like a squirrel in a cage, blinded by his own motion.

The Mess.

The messengers of hate are back.

On his sickbed of Saltpeter and Pity, Sloga had droned, "Max, the square, loudspeakers," his head cracked open by the fists of fascists on whom he'd trained the lethal screen of his Mac. Gabriel accelerated again. Who was Max? On which square were the loudspeakers spitting? Porte d'Aubervilliers, Porte de la Villette, Porte de Pantin, Porte de Bagnolet ... The left-wing "red" suburbs gave way to the right-wing "brown" ones—where the French fabricate Frenchness for little French people! Which square? The proud speakers of Marx Square? On his second pass, he crossed over streets crowded with commuters descending on the Porte des Lilas. Maybe Gégé, "the philosopher," would have the beginnings of an answer ...

Gilbert Gache, a philosophy professor who, due to a lack of imagination on the part of his contemporaries, had been saddled with the nickname Gégé, lived at the top end of Rue de Belleville, below a bakery that shared a wall with a Pakistani spice factory that serviced the Chinese restaurateurs at the bottom of the same street.

The scent of decaying fish, requisite base for the alchemy of *nuoc mam*, impregnated everything, even the voices of the divas trapped in the opera CDs that Gégé listened to while endlessly rereading the classics of Marxism and Freudian psychoanalysis. The perspective one subject provided to the other and vice versa plunged him into abysses of despair. The world would never be able to recover … So he never dove into the chasms of critical reasoning or the socialization of the libido without his provisions of Morgon, Chassagne-Montrachet, or de Pommard. What was most remarkable was that this combination of Freudian Marxism and suicidal alcoholism seemed to work well for him, and even at such a late hour, his discourse remained as clear as it was astute. He welcomed Gabriel as if they'd just seen each other the night before, when in fact it had been nearly three years since their last encounter.

Gégé had been runner-up for the championship title in French weightlifting while he was acing his high school literature exams, and he had maintained his truck-driver's build, which was a sensation in the classroom and helped recruit several student athletes to the side of Kierkegaard and Schopenhauer. He immediately filled two mustard jars with a ruby-colored Gevrey-Chambertin and cut off the whistling of a German diva with a tap to the stereo remote.

Gabriel duly complimented the quality of the wine before telling the hulky philosopher about Sloga's misfortunes, the book of quotations, Pedro's insights, his visit to the Gaston Lémoine offices, and finally, the events of earlier that evening, with the skinhead pressman, the kamikaze painter, and the ex-professional revolutionary turned fascist. Gégé listened to him without interrupting, leaning back in his chair, his eyes half-closed, his nose in the divine perfume of his Burgundy. When Gabriel had finished, with an account of Astrapov's impassioned call for a third World War, Gégé set down his glass and uttered this simple sentence:

—What surprises me is that this surprises you.

—Hold on! I'm not some naïf. With Le Pen and De Villiers attracting more than twenty percent in the presidential elections, we know that the trend toward authoritarianism isn't just about a few overzealous extremists … I've become complacent, relying on old assumptions: that the right will become more and more extreme … a sort of organic evolution. What I've discovered from Sloga's work is this massive ideological shift of certain people on the left, and not only the poor people in the projects, the ones who fall through the cracks … These are politicos, writers, journalists, profs …

Gilbert Gache refilled the jars of wine.

—We could talk for days about this: the loss of meaning, of social utility, the vanishing of points of reference … A simple experiment is enough to reveal the gravity of this crisis … I'd like to ask you to summarize for me, in just a few broad strokes, the platforms of the current strands of mainstream French thought … Gaullist, liberal, communist, socialist ... Go ahead ... Try to describe their platforms for me ...

Gabriel mumbled some vague concepts about equality, the new Europe, the strong franc, the protection of social benefits, competitiveness ...

—Now, try to do the same thing with the platform of the National Front ...

—France for the French, preferential treatment for citizens, the expulsion of immigrants, salaries for mothers paid for by the state, rejection of Maastricht, reestablishment of the death penalty, transfer of the ashes of Pét ...

Gégé had to stop him.

—You see? The results are irrefutable. On one side, a blurriness, a lack of ideological distinction, a long-term view ... On the other, crude notions hammered home, the demagogic but terribly effective precision of sloganeering, and miracle fixes ... We all have an irrepressible need to act on the world, to transform it. To think that our own weight can be enough to bend the common destiny. It's easy to transform this human quest into simple terms of war and winning, to name adversaries, even to invent them for the occasion ... Their greatest strength is that they promise instant change, they offer distraction from despair. You can't understand the fascist illusion if you lose sight of the fact that it's also a doctrine, a mystique. And one that works equally well on lost souls in the projects and on tenured professors!

Gabriel knew that Gégé was right. Still, he tried to play devil's advocate.

—The horror of the Nazi camps, the resistance, none of it was that long ago! There are limits to our moral ...

—Everything would be simpler if memory were a measurable, quantifiable thing ... For those who were deported, fifty years is like a day, maybe an hour ... For the little bastards you've just seen in action, it's an eternity, which is like saying it never happened. The other night I was watching a documentary about the eighth of May, 1945, in Sétif, when the French army deliberately massacred at least fifteen thousand Algerian rebels. An old Kabyle man was telling the story of how he'd come back from the European front, where he'd fought against the Nazis, to learn that his entire family had been executed. The journalist said to him: "After a half-century, the wound must have healed, though, hasn't it?" The peasant looked at him. After a moment, he responded: "In 1935, when I was ten years old, my schoolmaster, a Breton, taught us the history of France. He explained in detail the atrocities committed by the Prussians—he called them Krauts—during the war of 1870. It was more impressive to me than the tales about ogres and spirits that our elders told at bedtime ... This schoolmaster wasn't old, he was born with the century, and still he hadn't forgotten what he himself had not experienced: a war that took place thirty years before he came into the world! How do you expect me to forgive the murderers of my father, my mother, and my two brothers?"

Gilbert Gache granted himself a Burgundian respite. Gabriel took up the charge.

—Exactly! How can you justify the fact that the

communist papers are receptive to the writings of these fascistic morons? If anyone has fallen prey to the cult of repressed memories, it's them.

Gégé paused to fully appreciate a swallow of Chambertin, then set down his glass.

—First of all, I'm not justifying anything, especially in this domain. I'm trying to understand. Some people point out that it was easy for the National Front to take the Communist slogan "Made in France!" and add "by French workers!" as a way of appropriating it for their ends. That's not untrue. We can always find someone more nationalistic than we are. The real explanation is to be found elsewhere, in my opinion.

—Where, if I might ask?

—In '89!

—First you convince me that the Big Bang happened fifty years ago, and now you're going back to the French Revolution? Make up your mind!

—The year '89, if you've been paying attention, occurs once in each century ... So I will be more precise: 1989. The year of many dangers, when Gorbachev tried to forestall the implosion of his empire by letting go of Poland, of Czechoslovakia and East Germany, with the incandescent symbol of the Berlin Wall as it fell ... For years, no one but the most naïve and fanatical still believed in the existence of the "socialist system," in the "worker's homeland" ... The Revolution became like Lenin's mummy rotting away in its mausoleum-sarcophagus, with armies of scholars still attempting to dust it off. As if we needed the body of Nietzsche to make use of his ideas—what impoverished thinking! There is really no one more religious than materialists!

—And '89? Haven't we strayed?

—If you require a readymade discourse, go back to your skinheads and their commandant Gregovic ... Dialogue is thought in action ...

—Gavrovic, not Gregovic ...

—I stand corrected: Gavrovic ... The higher-ups of the French Communist Party were worried that the ground-swell wouldn't spare them, that the party would disinte-grate ... The majority tried to save what they could. Some moved quickly and rejoined the socialists, some became "re"-something or other ... Re-founders, re-constructors, renovators ... Others caught in the shipwreck latched onto any plank that floated within reach. The more rotten, the better. Among them there was, of course, Kevin Kervan's *Continental Furor* ... The outlet for a generation of earnest imitators of Céline, Drieu la Rochelle, Brasillach ... Writers who live by proxy. It existed for this small faction, and the result was a commingling of communist and fascist bylines. An adjunct secretary general of the C.G.T. rubbed shoul-ders with the editor in chief of the far-right journal *Présent*, the director of a communist publishing house sat down with anti-Semitic pamphleteer Mac Daube, the members of the central committee of the Communist Party signed editori-als that appeared below racist cartoons by the caricaturist from the *National Weekly*! And in a single month, Ivan As-trapov gave his chronicles on Yugoslavia to both the fascist monthly *Shock* and the communist weekly *Revolution*. One of the editorial writers for *Humanity*, Pierre Jumel, who is said to have foresight, was repeatedly accused of anti-Semitism, was even condemned by the court more than once, I believe … It wasn't until the communist "intellectuals" invited the founding philosopher of the New Right, also the director of a fascistic review, to a colloquium on "the renaissance of critical thinking" at the Institute of Marxist Research that a scandal finally erupted in their ranks.

Gilbert Gache stood up to open the window. The smell of decomposing fish wafted into the room. Gabriel pulled the fabric of his shirt to his nose.

—China awakens! Do you believe that any of them would be idiotic enough to bust the head of a forgotten writer looking into the subject six years after all this happened?

—It's unlikely. As long as the relative majority of the Communist Party has moved into a relatively clean house … Maurice Céninf, its Number Two, was put in forced retirement; the official poet, Frederic Romanescu, now works as a private editor under the name Merle the Mockingbird; and *Revolution*, the communist paper that gathered up the largest portion of the drifters, has simply been scuttled.

—So that's not where we need to be looking …

Gégé closed the window and took advantage of his upright position to open a sumptuous Clos-Vougeot.

—We'll let it breathe for a minute. If we don't, it'll be worse than these intellectual atrocities! I don't know. You can't rule out an act of individual will. Men are always more complicated than the most astute theories about them … I don't want to compete with you, but a philosopher is, in a way, a detective of thought … On one side, the commies have cleaned house, though not exactly a full spring cleaning; on the other side, the fascists need public struggles to demonstrate their powers of seduction ... Sloga isn't causing them any problems. So you may as well not tax your neurons in either of these directions ...

—So what's left?

The philosopher brought his nose expectantly to a point just above the neck of the wine bottle.

—A clandestine conductor ... An underground orchestra ... There are those who are impatient, who fold their hand as soon as their luck turns, and others who bluff with a grin on their faces ... Agents in waiting. Imagine that your novelist had fallen in with some people who were above suspicion; who were preparing, tranquilly, under cover of their reputations, the coming of a new order ... People get bludgeoned for that, and I think they even get killed!

He placed his hand on the label of the Clos-Vougeot and tipped the bottle toward the mustard jars.

It was almost ten o'clock the next morning when Gabriel awoke on a mattress nestled between piles of books on psychology, philosophy, and sociology. Gilbert Gache had pinned a note to the door to inform him that the stash of Burgundy was in a niche in the middle of the landing beneath the stairway, and that, in addition, all he had to do was push the button on the coffee machine for a dose of Arabica.

18

FINAL PROOFS

The previous night's storm had washed the sidewalks of Paris clean. The air, cool and fresh, perfumed the plane trees, the soil, and the wet grass. Gabriel waited for the traffic warden to finish filling out her ticket and proceed to the next victim before he took his place behind the wheel of the Peugeot. The army of enforcers had been uncannily effective all day: the Minister of the Interior would only need to consult their duplicates to know, to the hour, the details of Gabriel's movements. He drove back up Rue de Bellville to the Porte des Lilas and hopped onto the ring road for a stretch, just for fun. The library at the Pitié-Salpêtrière was taking the day off, as was the nurse of chapters and verses. He went directly to Intensive Care, carrying his red and brown evidence in a shopping bag. The young doctor on duty informed him that André Sloga had been transferred to a regular unit, as his condition, judged to be satisfactory, now required little more than careful supervision. He directed Gabriel to the appropriate wing. The dragon lady who was watching over Sloga and a dozen other delicate cases followed regulations with a tenacity against which Gabriel had to muster buried stores of energy.

—Monsieur Sloga has suffered an extremely violent

head trauma. He is just beginning to remember bits and pieces of his recent past. What he needs now is absolute and total calm ...

Gabriel held up the manuscript of *Moon over the Marshes*, the assorted notes, the dictionary of citations.

—I repeat, I am his private secretary ... This manuscript absolutely must be submitted to the publisher before the end of the week, so the book can be in stores at the beginning of October ... He just needs to sign off on the final proofs.

He approached the Tatar and lowered his voice, taking on a confidential tone.

—It's on the official shortlist for the Goncourt ...

He could feel her being swayed.

—If he comes to his senses in two or three days and finds out that the publication of his book has been postponed until after prize season, I'm afraid there's a real possibility he could relapse ...

Gabriel hadn't completely convinced her, but she didn't want to risk being responsible for a literary disaster of such proportions.

—Fine. You can go in. Five minutes, not one second more. You ask him to sign, and you leave immediately.

André Sloga turned his head toward the door. He smiled at Gabriel.

—Is it you, doctor?

The detective drew the visitor's chair close to the bed.

—I'm not with the hospital. My name is Gabriel Lecouvreur, and I'm trying to find the people who attacked you ...

Sloga took a deep breath.

—I was attacked, are you sure? You must be mistaken. They are very nice here. I can't remember ...

—You're in a hospital, and for good reason. You were found in the parking lot of your building, on Rue Jeanne d'Arc. Your assailants fled, and I want to know who they were ...

—Why? Are you with the police?

Gabriel saw the surveillante's nose pause at the window and then move away.

—No, I'm just one of your readers. I saw in the paper what had happened to you, and it stuck in my throat ... You do remember that you're a writer, I hope ...

—I don't know if that's a good thing ...

He touched his forehead.

—Maybe that's the thing I should have erased!

—Don't say that ... I've read at least four of your books, *The Innocents*, *Hell's Harvest*, *Weekend in Nagasaki*, *Counter-current* ... I've also taken a look at your latest manuscript, *Moon over the Marshes* ...

André Sloga shifted his weight to his elbows so he could lift his head higher onto the pillow.

—*Moon over the Marshes?* You must be mistaken, I would never have chosen such a ridiculous title ...

Gabriel took the manuscript from his lap and opened it at random.

—No, I'm not mistaken ... There's not a single sentence in here that could have been written by anyone else! It's pure Sloga! Listen ... "There's a major arcana in the tarot deck that shows two wolves howling at the moon, from which droplets of blood fall between two enormous towers that mark the boundaries of consciousness, while a crayfish dives into a deep body of water. It's the moon, but it represents fear; it's as old as the planet ... And so man remembers that he must die."

He had glanced up between two sentences and seen Sloga's lips mouth the shapes of the words. He turned a few pages.

—"The only signs of life. All the rest had plunged into eternity: the starry sky wreathed with clouds, the contrasting shades of silver and ink in the humble duck pond, the moist sand that slowed the steps of bare feet ..."

The writer lip-synched the words the instant Gabriel pronounced them, as if tracing a path in his memory.

—I have the feeling that I memorized this text a long time ago, a very long time ago ... and you're saying that it's mine?

—Yes, it's your next novel ... Do you remember Max, on the square ... Loudspeakers?

His face lit up like a child's.

—No, but that's odd ... Is that also mine?

—You wouldn't stop repeating those words after you'd regained consciousness ... I don't know if they have something to do with the attack on you, but what's clear to me is that whoever beat you up did so to make you give up your investigations into the collusion between communist intellectuals and politicians and their fascist counterparts ... I have a whole series of quotations here that you took from books, from journals like *Continental Furor* ...

Sloga painfully furrowed his brow.

—It's all very blurry ... Buried. Buried deeply ... You could read me a bit ...

Gabriel selected an excerpt from an article in the *Shock of the Month*, July 1992.

—You didn't record the names of the authors, but I have a feeling that this one is by Ivan Astrapov, a former painter and Soviet dissident ... Here's what he wrote: "We may talk about a flirtation between nationalists and communists in France, but in Russia this alliance is already a reality, in politics and in daily life. On February 23, 1992, opposition forces on Tverskaya Street in Moscow faced off against Yeltsin's militia, waving flags that were nationalist, monarchist, and Red! ... We are living in an era of radical changes of allegiance; everywhere new barricades are being constructed, and we defend these barricades with new brothers in arms ... Would you like to see the new red-and-brown flag of the nationalist-communist movement?"

The nurse peered around the half-open door. André Sloga raised his hand to reassure her. He waited until she had disappeared, then looked intently at his visitor.

—My brain is in pieces ... They wreaked havoc on my neurons ... There are names, phrases, that awaken images, but they're surrounded by a void ... Since this morning, I have been able to see, with incredible precision, whole scenes from my childhood: when my father brought me with him to anarchist meetings, where he played the accordion ... The songs are stuck in my head now, every last note ... There are also lots of things about Spain, the departure of the Brigades from Barcelona, the Olympic protests ... The resistance ...

The closer I get to the present moment, the more foggy it becomes ... Read that sentence to me again, the one where he talks about the flags ...

—"Would you like to see the new red-and-brown flag of the nationalist-communist movement?" That one?

He lowered his eyelids to focus on Astrapov's question. His jaw muscles bulged from the intensity of the effort. He started to sputter.

—I know, I know, but I don't know where anymore ... Wait, wait, I remember that painter ... I met him in a bookstore, in Paris ... There were paintings on the wall ... They were all there ...

Gabriel drew closer still.

—Which bookstore? And *they*, who are they?

Sloga, drained, opened his eyes. He caught his breath.

—I bought books there, lots of books ... They're in my library, at my house ... Take the key, in the armoire ...

The dragon lady looked demonstratively at her watch when Gabriel exited the writer's room.

—I said five minutes.

—I'm sorry, he had to correct two or three things ... You know how they are ...

19

CHAINS ON THE CHASSIS

Just for an extra thrill, Gabriel opened the door to 2 Rue Jeanne d'Arc using the skeleton key from the captain of the fire station on Rue de la Pompe, even though he had André Sloga's keys in his hand. An old woman with a face like an angry tortoise emerged from the elevator, cursing at the universe. She looked the detective up and down before addressing him authoritatively.

—Where are you going?

—To your place, now that there's no one else in there!

She spun around to step back into the elevator, but she was too slow: the door closed on her wrinkled nose.

Sloga's name was engraved on a small plaque mounted on the door, but Gabriel didn't need to read it to know that he had found the writer's apartment. A series of dents in the jamb were evidence that the security door had been forced. He cautiously pushed it open.

Steel-backed wood scraped against the papers that were strewn across the carpet. Gabriel stepped inside to take stock of the extent of the disaster. All of the shelves had been emptied of their books; drawers had been thrown to the floor; file folders had been opened, their contents dispersed. The linen closet and the cleaning supply closet had met a similar fate … He recalled the presence of Inspector Vergeat, the day of his first visit to Rue Jeanne d'Arc, and for a split second he suspected the Bureau of Investigation. He instantly rejected this theory. Their highly specialized search teams had long ago abandoned such crude techniques.

One of his few journalist friends had told him how his cat had proved beyond a doubt that his apartment had been visited by "plumbers." He had a Chartreux that was agoraphobic and neurasthenic, that hadn't put a paw outside the apartment in five years and that exhibited signs of extreme anxiety whenever the jounralist so much as opened a window. When returning home one night, he'd found the cat, in shock, sitting on the welcome mat—while he had a clear memory of caressing her, as she lolled on her cushion, before going out. Nothing had been moved in the apartment, not a particle of dust had been displaced, but everything had been inspected. Some person had entered as discreetly as a ghost, and for reasons that were obscure to the journalist, the cat had followed that person out the door.

The situation at Sloga's was entirely different. Whoever was responsible for this pillaging was not looking for anything, except to make the writer lay down his arms the very moment he returned home from the hospital. Gabriel gathered up a pile of books, an armful of file folders, then another, then again another, and then, discouraged, he flopped onto the chair across from Sloga's desk. The writer had jotted down ideas, names, and references on Post-its that he had stuck to an old map of the world on which conquered countries and fallen empires still existed, but none of the little yellow squares revealed the slightest hidden meaning.

Though he was probably unaware of it, Sloga suffered from the same disorder as Louis Aragon: he could not let go of postcards, invitations, photos people had sent him. The walls of the hallway that led to the bedroom were covered with such souvenirs, held in place by multicolor pushpins, the wallpaper no longer visible except high up near the crown molding. There were scenes of Venice, of Saint Raphaël; reproductions of works by Picasso and Edward Hopper; invitations to plays and concerts, photos by Doisneau and Willy Ronis; pacifist stickers, remnants of an activist past; a few press clippings ... Gabriel had paused at a small mosaic made from exotic stamps when Astrapov's name caught his eye. It was printed in large white letters on a black card tacked below the light switch.

La Caillera bookstore &

Éditions de la Vielle Gauffre

invite you to meet

PIERRE JUMEL

on June 21, 1995, starting at 6:00 p.m.

34 Rue de Colonel Henry

to celebrate the release of his book

FROM ONE EXTREME TO ANOTHER

alongside an exhibition of "World of Ends"

the last paintings of

IVAN ASTRAPOV

Gabriel pried the thumbtack out with his fingernails and turned the card over. André Sloga had copied down the date of the event along with a single observation: "They're all here." The detective found some tools beneath the sink and improvised a crude lock to secure the door. The neighbor was waiting for him at the elevator, flanked by an old man who abandoned any plan for recrimination upon seeing the size of the detective.

Gabriel had passed by the La Caillera bookstore before, halfway up the hill to the Butte aux Cailles on the other side of Avenue d'Italie; he may even have patronized it. He left the Peugeot near the imposing Church of Saint Anne and walked back up Rue Buot. He turned at the corner; the shop, with its shelves of cheap used books, was only twenty meters away. He kept walking, lost in his thoughts, composing lines of dialogue appropriate for a book shopper that would allow him, without giving himself away, to bring up the true object of his curiosity.

When he looked up, he discovered that Francis, the skinhead printer, was waiting for him just up the block. He was sitting on his Moto Becane next to another motorcycling warrior for the cause, also with shaved head, cargo pants, and Doc Martens. Francis pointed at Gabriel and scowled. The motorcycle engines roared, and it was clear to Gabriel that Francis no longer saw him as a potential contributor to Éditions Gaston Lémoine, or as a soldier for Greater Serbia. He turned on his heels and started back down Rue Buot. The motorcycles bounded onto the sidewalk, slalomed between parked cars ... He could see that he had neither the time nor the breath to reach his car. He rifled through his pocket without slowing his pace, flattened himself suddenly against a tall carriage door, and inserted the key to the city into the lock below the electronic keypad.

Miraculously, the door gave way, and he emerged into a paved courtyard which he sprinted across, diving into the stairwell on the other side. The two skinheads banged on the thick wood, and Gabriel could hear the idling of motors. He slinked up a few steps, opened a window and climbed out into a narrow passageway littered with ancient refrigerators, dismembered pieces of furniture, and a gate that opened into the gardens of the Church of Saint Anne. Gabriel waved at two priests who were playing badminton on the rectory lawn. He allowed himself a few minutes of rest in the church nave, enough to catch his breath between a devotee kneeling in ecstasy in front of the bust of Saint Arvor and a cleaning woman polishing the prayer benches while singing the Serge Lama song *"Je suis malade."*

He crossed the small, somber funeral crowd climbing the steps to the church's main facade on Rue Bobillot. The Peugeot was fifteen meters away, and he made a run for it. As soon as he was at the wheel, Francis's motorcycle pulled up next to his door. The skinhead was holding his chain lock like a flail. He started beating it against the car, and the driver-side window exploded into shards. Without thinking, Gabriel shifted into first gear. The Peugeot lurched out of its spot, taking with it a taillight from the car in front, and knocking over the printer's bike. The accomplice was waiting in ambush at the corner of Rue du Moulinet. Gabriel charged at him, and the skinhead had no choice but to leap from his seat a fraction of a second before the car's tires crushed his front wheel.

Francis didn't relent. He gunned his engine and caught up to Gabriel, flinging the chain at him through the shattered window. Gabriel ran the red light at the intersection of Tolbiac and fled toward Avenue d'Italie. The skinhead printer backed off as soon as they had left the maze of narrow streets in the Butte-aux-Cailles. Now all he could do was monitor the movements of his prey and wait for an opportune moment to swoop down on him.

Gabriel drove around the Place d'Italie and turned onto Boulevard de l'Hôpital. He slammed on the brakes and pulled up behind the prefecture of the 13th Arrondissement. The tires wailed on the hot asphalt. The two officers on duty outside the precinct rushed over just in time to see a motorcyclist pull up alongside a beaten-up Peugeot and rap on the roof with a chain while the driver escaped through the passenger door. When he saw the cops, the rider reared his bike and disappeared in the direction of Avenue des Gobelins.

Gabriel lost a good part of the afternoon responding to questions from the cops, who, once they were made aware of the extraordinary nature of his activities, had put a call in to the Bureau. A junior Vergeat must have instructed them not to let him off easy. He stuck to his story: the biker had reacted explosively when Gabriel didn't let him into his lane. The inspector who was presiding over the hearing didn't believe a word of it. Sneering, he let Gabriel go at the end of his shift, just before four o'clock.

—You may return to your wreck ... One of my men

took down the motorcycle's license plate, but it didn't make it into the report. If the insurance company asks for it, for the reimbursement, don't worry ... Come see us ... You tell us what really happened, we give you the number.

He'd driven barely ten meters when one of the cops pulled him over. He circled around the car and issued two tickets: one for failing to signal, and the other for not wearing a seatbelt. Gabriel picked up the stack of citations he'd been collecting for three days and showed it to the officer.

—Just put it on top, I'm going for the world record.

The public servant's cap trembled with righteous pleasure. He wrote out a third ticket, for insulting a representative of the state.

20

LA CAILLERA

Gabriel drove by the hair salon several times, but couldn't work up the courage to show Cheryl the state of her Peugeot. He left it behind a garden on Rue Désiré-Préaux in Montreuil, in an unofficial garage managed by a former bookstore owner who had sunk his business by refusing to sell Zaraï and Jardin, Sulitzer and Giroud. Now the former bookseller fixed fenders under the table and restored wrecked cars to their factory shades of paint.

The metro, packed with just-returned vacationers, smelled like the end of beach season, a subtle mixture of suntan oil and sweat. The train stopped for a security alert a hundred meters past the Place d'Italie, and a wino, jarred awake by the absence of the sound of wheels on tracks, got up to relieve himself against the hermetically sealed door. It was nearly eight o'clock when Gabriel emerged from the Corvisart station. The neighborhood's restaurants, run by anarchists-turned-entrepreneurs, were filling up with customers. Buskers sang Ferré, Brassens, Bruant, occasionally Montéhus—as opposed to any truly subversive music that might interfere with digestion. Gabriel indulged the cravings aroused by the restaurants' aromas with a crepe bought from a kiosk in front of the Vallès-Burger, and walked back down toward Avenue Colonel Henri. The bookseller had just brought in the used book bins and was lowering the security grate on La Caillera. Gabriel stooped slightly and entered the shop.

—I'm closing up ...

Gabriel didn't turn around. He pretended to be studying the titles on a shelf as he scanned the store to make sure nobody else was inside. Classic anarchist texts rubbed shoulders with re-issues of Rebatet, Brasillach, Abel Bonnard.

—I won't be long. I've got nothing to read tonight ...

The bookseller came back inside. He removed the exterior door handle, closed the door, and stowed away the crank for the grate.

—You should have said it was an emergency ...

In a nook that was invisible to passersby, Gabriel had glimpsed a post-war edition of the most disturbing book in Paul Morand's oeuvre, *Sweet France*. He put down the Série Noir paperbacks he'd been flipping through.

—I'm going to take one or two of these, but I've also been looking for a long time for an out-of-print book by Paul Morand ...

—Which one?

—*Sweet France* ... I haven't been able to get my hands on it ...

The bookseller beamed.

—It's your lucky day: a copy of that just came in ... It's the third printing, first edition ... The only thing is, it's not cheap ...

—I'd love to see it. Do you accept credit cards?

He locked the cash register and put the keys in his pocket, then headed toward the back of the store and climbed up two rungs of a ladder to reach for the book. Gabriel followed him. He waited until the bookseller's balance wavered, then violently jabbed his kidneys with the end of a size-16 socket wrench that he'd borrowed from the mechanic in Montreuil.

—You will descend calmly, without turning around, and you will put your hands flat against the wall … That's it … We aren't turning around, right?

The merchant was up against the wall, and Gabriel spread out his legs and gave his ankles a few brisk swipes with the wrench.

—I had a feeling you were going to pull something …The keys to the register are in my left pocket, but you'll be disappointed, we empty it out three times a day … There's almost nothing in there …

Gabriel let him finish his speech. Continuing to press the wrench against his kidneys, he used his other hand to undo the bookseller's belt and the two top buttons of his jeans, which fell to his knees. The guy flipped out: What the hell was about to happen to his backside? He tried turning his head but Gabriel drew a palm briskly across his jaw.

—You're insane … What is it you want?

—You know Francis?

—Who?

—Francis. You know, from *Top Model*, the skinhead edition …

—I don't know what you're talking about …

Gabriel shoved his face against the wall and grabbed him by the hair.

—You were talking to him and his twin brother just this

afternoon ... I'm looking for him, I need to make a police report ...

—I don't have his address ... All I know is that he works at Gaston Lémoine, in Gennevilliers ... Are you the red Peugeot?

—Nobody's ever called me that before, but I'll accept it ... It's a bit strange to be confused with a heap of metal, but it's not particularly insulting. I'm going to tell you what I want to know, and you're going to answer me without trying to get away. You and those henchmen, you beat the hell out of one of my very old friends, and ever since, he's been trying to reassemble the pieces of his mind, just a few steps away from here, at the Pitié ... Sloga, André Sloga, does that ring a bell?

He shrugged.

—I'm a bookseller ... Of course I know him ... We carry his books ...

Gabriel closed his free fist and struck it squarely against the ear of his hostage, who staggered from the blow.

—I'm not talking to the bookseller. I'm asking the guy who's pals with Astrapov, Jumel, Somporc, Kevin Keran, Thierry Tegret, Bucar ...

—I don't understand ...

The end of the wrench dug into the bookseller's calf. He staggered and almost fell, catching his feet in his lowered pants.

—I believe I've already told you that I don't have a lot of time ... I know that Sloga came here, that he even took part in some events ... I want to know who decided to beat him up, and most of all, why!

The man remained silent. With his giant hand, Gabriel picked up the first volume of the *Encyclopedia of French Rights* and brought it down on his head, then he probed each vertebra with the mouth of the wrench.

—Listen, I'm prepared to leave you in the same state in which your friends left André Sloga in the parking lot on Rue Jeanne d'Arc ... First, I'll put a bullet in your spinal column. Not high enough to miss the cord ... Right about here ... Can you feel the barrel of my gun? That'll do enough harm to put you in a wheelchair for the rest of your days ... You'll have all the time in the world to remember this evening, and to regret not having talked...

The bookseller was starting to be convinced.

—But what do you want me to tell you? I don't understand what you want ...

—First of all, the simplest thing ... Who was it who beat up Sloga?

—I don't know exactly ... It was guys from Francis's gang ... Skinheads ...

—Well, all right then. Seems to me that a bit of scalp massaging has a good effect on you, it revives your neurons ... Did you meet Sloga here in the store?

—Yes ... He bought a bunch of books from us, for about a year ... Mostly stuff from the 1930s ... Léon Daudet, Abel Bonnard, Robert Brasillach ... Since we came from the same movement, anarchism, we gradually integrated him into our group and introduced him to the young writers who share our ideas ...

—And what are your ideas?

—This isn't really the moment to talk politics ...

A jab with the wrench changed his mind.

—There has been a truce between the forces of capitalism and the world's pseudo-revolutionary organizations. And this partnership depends on the biggest lie of all time: the legend of the gas chambers ...

—Explain this to me ... I'm a simple man. I don't see the connection ...

The bookseller was bold enough to let out a sigh.

—America and Israel can perpetrate any conceivable abuse on their people, as long as the absolute, unsurpassable crime remains the purported genocide of the Jews ... Until this myth is dispelled, no real revolution will be possible ...

Someone on the street stopped at the shop window and thumped on it. The bookseller started to cry for help. The only response he got was a forearm blow to the crook of his neck, stopping the cries in his throat. The onlooker gave up and went on his way.

—I told you to stay quiet! Your analysis stinks of shit. The problem is that it's laid out in black and white in your publications, and the fact that André heard it spoken out loud isn't what got him bludgeoned to within an inch of his life. There has to be something else ...

Gabriel was forced to make use of the *Encyclopedia of French Rights* again to jog the memory of the bookseller, who abandoned at last any form of resistance.

—We trusted him completely, and we made the mistake, one night, of inviting him here at the same time as an important person in our movement, who spoke unguardedly of the ideas we all shared ... When we learned that

Sloga was in fact an infiltrator, we had no choice but to shut him up ...

—And, if you don't mind my asking, who let the cat out of the bag?

—A friend who heads up the Asphalt Noir imprint at the publishing house where Sloga was hoping to publish his book ...

—And the important person, who was it?

The merchant shook his head from right to left, then right to left.

—I can't, it's not possible ...

Another massive blow to the jaw.

—I'm afraid you don't have a choice ...

He sputtered out the name.

—It's Jean Brienne ...

—Jean Brienne! *The* Brienne, from the dictionaries?

—Yes ... Sloga's plan was to reveal everything tomorrow, at the worst possible moment ... It couldn't wait ...

—Tomorrow! Really! Tomorrow ... Now I understand everything ...

He grabbed the bookseller by the collar, forced him to turn around, and showed him the socket wrench just as he crushed his liver with a sucker punch. The shopkeeper was down for the count, surrounded by the somber covers of tomes by Bonnard, Rebatet, Suarez, Brasillach, Carrel, Astrapov and Jumel. Before leaving, Gabriel picked up a Charyn and a Vilar that had no business in such company, but left the Malet behind.

21

THE DEFINITION OF A KRAUT

Gabriel had jumped into a taxi that let him out on the Quai Sisley, in Villeneuve-la-Garenne. He'd continued on foot to Pedro's docked barge, drawing growls from the neighborhood dogs. There, he'd explained the results of his investigations and revealed the name of the man who had ordered the attack on André Sloga in order to protect his career. Pedro had immediately set about creating a complete identity for him as a journalist: passport, professional tricolor press pass, business cards from the Japanese magazine *Hori-Shimbun*, letter of affiliation from the Institute ... Mid-morning, with a Boyard in his mouth, he'd driven Gabriel to Rue Popincourt, where Cheryl shaved him and did his hair under the watchful eyes of the assistant's Yorkie; then, after a light lunch at the Pied de Porc, they'd gone by car as far as the Louvre, where they parked within sight of its famous glass pyramid.

They'd walked together to the Seine, where the militant counterfeiter gestured across the river to the roof of the building which, if he remembered correctly, a dying Cocteau had described as the hull of an old ship anchored on the riverbank.

—They never begin their sacraments before three

o'clock, and it's best if you don't show up too early, to avoid being recognized ... Once you're there, you hold tight for a good half hour, and then, when you're ready, you get to work. Take a deep breath, say your piece, and bust the head of the first person who tries to stop you ... Don't be afraid, they aren't used to anyone getting physical ...

Then he'd slapped Gabriel on the back and smiled.

—¡Venceremos!

Gabriel crossed the Seine on the Pont des Arts and set a determined foot on the Quai Conti. He walked up to the small door to the right of the Coupole's main entrance, where members of the Republican Guard in ceremonial dress were saluting the Academicians as they came in. Gabriel held out his phony invitation and accreditation papers to the usher, who handed him a white card with a seat number on it. He went up the ornate stairs, each step of which was graced with a guard in his finery, briefly ogled the breasts of a nude statue, and entered the circular hall. The members of the committee were taking their seats on the bench, accompanied by drum rolls.

At exactly three o'clock, Maurice Druon, the Perpetual Secretary of the Académie Française, stood up.

—The meeting is now in session. I'll hand over the floor to Monsieur Jean Brienne for his acceptance speech.

Jean Brienne, in grandiose attire, sword at his side, rose from his seat in the second-to-last row reserved for members of the fellowship. Several dozen photographers crowded around him to immortalize the Academician-elect.

When the chaos had subsided, he put on his glasses and began to read into the microphone the first page of an homage to Edgar Faure, whose death made him inheritor of his seat. He attempted a joke to begin with.

—The thing I'll always remember about my illustrious predecessor is his barbed tongue, in such contrast with his perfectly smooth head ...

Gabriel waited for the first quarter of an hour, observing the audience. Everyone who mattered in media and culture was there: acerbic critics, complacent publishers, ancient journalists and young philosophers sitting elbow to elbow, writers on a quest for respectability, members of the black literati gazing at the radiant faces of the Immortals* who represented the hard-won effects of their labors ... Gabriel waited until Jean Brienne had finished recounting his predecessor's life in politics and started in on his calamitous career as a detective novelist under the pseudonym Edgar Sanday. He rose from his seat and barged through a hedge of officials, jostling a dozen people before the photographers noticed the growing disruption. They aimed their zooms and flashes, and continued to click away at the detective while he posed for an instant beside the Academician-to-be, who was still in the midst of his speech. Then, with an imperial gesture, he snatched the man's extra-credit report from his hands. Michel Droit and Alain Peyrefitte, in defense of their future colleague, lunged at him, but Gabriel

---

* Members of the Académie Française are known as Immortals because they are elected for life, although expulsion for grave misconduct is permitted. Several members were expelled after World War II for their association with the collaborationist Vichy regime.

Lecouvreur took them on just as Pedro would have wanted him to, issuing a resounding slap to the jaw of the former, for May '68, and a jab with the wrench between the legs of the latter, for the elephants of Africa. Gabriel grabbed the nominee by the embroidered collar of his green suit, and started to pull him toward the exit. Jean Brienne managed, though with unseemly effort, to draw his sword. He lunged toward his attacker, brandishing the gleaming blade. Gabriel simply shifted his hips and the musketeer lay knocked out at his feet.

Before the Republican Guard could get to him, Gabriel was able to grab the microphone. As they dragged him away, he yelled into it:

—The person who really deserves this elegy is still alive … Nobody here knows his name … André Sloga … He's fighting to recover the memory that too many of us have lost, thanks to trash like Jean Brienne … *Bon appétit, Monsieurs!*

The police threw him in a cell for forty-eight hours for forged credentials, after charging him without due process. Cheryl was not there when he got home to Rue Popincourt. She was out on a call, setting an elderly home-bound client's curls. She had left the mail on the table with the Marilyn Monroe tablecloth. He glanced quickly at the envelopes, opening the one with a return-address stamp from the *Voice of the Marshes*. In chicken-scratch handwriting, Fred Ledoeunf, the journalist from Fontenay-le-Comte, informed him that he had just submitted his resignation and that, to boot, he was quitting the profession altogether. Gabriel had to squint to decipher the deformed letters:

The reason for this decision is that the Bonvix police have just arrested Valérie Audiat's slayer, who is guilty beyond a shadow of a doubt. He has confessed to everything, providing details that no one but the murderer could know. It turns out to have been the sadistic crime of a true predator. I have grossly misrepresented the facts, and I am here to accept the consequences. It is not only myself I have misled: by virtue of my position in the community, I have shared my delusion with many thousands of readers. Since my arrival at the *Voice of the Marshes*, I have allowed myself to wallow in the mud of corruption; I have forsworn critical thinking; I've abandoned myself to the opinions of every other "well-meaning" citizen. It should be stated for the record that Valérie Audiat entered the profession of nursing out of a desire to be of service to others. The doctors, pharmacists, and veterinarians of the region caught their deadly disease through independent means, and the aging Audiat died of grief, a man broken from years of slander. I have included in this letter the affidavit of the killer. If you could share it with André Sloga, so that he may make the necessary modifications to his manuscript, you would be doing me a great service …

The Octopus folded the letter, slipped it into his pocket, and left the hair salon for the Pitié.

22

MAX, ON THE SQUARE

Éloi, the village sage, insists to this day that when a storm hits la Bastide, the rain spares Serviès. It had been dousing other, dryer villages, far from the Val de Dagne. The last tourists had left the region a good two months ago, and the grape harvest had taken place the week before, filling the barrels with what old-timers were already touting as one of the best vintages since the War.

Sitting beneath an arbor in front of a pastis, Max knew that nobody would be coming back to this remote part of Corbières before next summer. He had come to close up his family's inn, *Chez Verdier*, for the winter, except for one or two rooms that would be kept up for the occasional passing boar hunter or traveling salesman. The grizzly sounds of an old Plastic Bertrand record began to play over the loud-speakers, with Jeannine's voice rising above the static:

—Attention, please! Monsieur Jean-Claude Gibert, the butcher from Lagrasse, has arrived on the square ... Today you have a choice of beef, fresh sausage, and venison stewed in Corbière ... Attention, please! The butcher from Lagrasse has arrived on the square ...

Max opened the *Indépendent de Pérpignan* that his wife had brought back from the bakery along with a loaf of bread. He skimmed the local news, pausing to read the weather report, and then noticed a photograph in the Arts & Culture section. He recognized the old man who had stayed with them for three weeks in August, the one who was so interested in their local hero, Joseph Délteil, for whom one of the village's wines had been named. He called to his wife, who came and leaned over his shoulder.

—I don't have my glasses ... What's it saying about him?

—I never would have thought it, he was such a simple man, but Monsieur Sloga is a writer ... His latest book just came out from Éditions Baleine ... It's called *Moon over the Marshes* ...

—What kind of book is it?

—According to this, it's a tragic love story ...

The Plastic Bertrand record started up again.

—Attention, please! The fishmonger from Sigean has arrived on the square ... Today's sale item is sardines ... Attention, please! The fishmonger from Sigean has arrived on the square ...

Max turned to his wife.

—I've got a hankering for sardines for lunch ... How about you?

—Yes, me too, but don't get too many, like last time. They don't freeze well at all ...

She walked away, and the first drops fell on the arbor, as if for the sole purpose of giving Éloi the lie.

AN INTERVIEW WITH DIDIER DAENINCKX

What inspired you to write *Nazis in the Metro*?

I wrote this book in 1995, just after the Yugoslav Wars that killed more than 250,000 people in Europe. A very strange phenomenon was taking place then: French intellectuals from the extreme left were defending ultranationalist killers. People like the French-Russian writer Edouard Limonov enlisted in the Serbian army, and then came to the fashionable bars of Saint-Germain in Paris boasting of their triumphs. It was that climate, that shift in the elite classes, that I wanted to describe.

***Nazis in the Metro* tells the story of a writer called André Sloga. Was he modeled on anyone?**

Yes, I modeled him on a writer friend of mine by the name of Jean Meckert (1910–1995), who published numerous crime novels under the pseudonym Jean Amila. He was violently attacked in the 1970s and lost his memory as a result. He later carried out investigations into his own life, in order to recover the memories he had lost.

What drives your detective, Gabriel Lecouvreur?

He has a major flaw for the times we live in: he is devoid of indifference, he's affected by the suffering of others. If he were a philosopher, he would define himself as an "Unhappy Consciousness." Which doesn't stop him from wanting to put everything to rights!

Why do you so often take real historical and political events as the basis of your novels?

I think history invited itself into my cradle: I had one pacifist grandfather who was a deserter in the First World War; one communist grandfather who was the mayor of a town near Paris in 1935 and who resigned in protest of the Hitler-Stalin pact; a mother who used to travel secretly into Franco's Spain to work with those plotting to overthrow the dictator; a bedroom that served as a hiding place for Vietcong emissaries during the secret negotiations that took place in Paris in the middle of the Vietnam war ... I had no choice but to investigate all of that, this family history of fighting injustice, of solidarity with people from far away.

You're known as one of France's most outspoken writers. Have you ever experienced an attack like that on Sloga in *Nazis in the Metro***?**

A few years ago, an extreme-right group, Unité Radicale, tried to kill President Jacques Chirac on the Champs-Élysées in Paris during a military parade. The police found a file on me in this group's records—my address, telephone number, a write-up of my movements ... Later, someone emptied many liters of gas on my front door and set it alight. Fortunately, my neighbors alerted me, and my wife and I were able to escape. Periods of crisis don't tend to calm such passions ...

MORE BY FRANCE'S LEADING POLITICAL CRIME WRITER

MURDER IN MEMORIAM

"Serves as a tap on the shoulder—
a necessary reminder that what is
dead is not buried, and what is
buried is, unfortunately, not dead."
—DEREK RAYMOND,
AUTHOR OF
THE FACTORY SERIES

$14.95 U.S./Can.
Paperback: 978-1-61219-146-1
Ebook: 978-1-61219-147-8

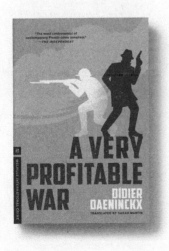

A VERY PROFITABLE WAR

"One hell of an unflinching
look at war and its aftermath."
—*THE THRILLING
DETECTIVE*

$14.95 U.S./Can.
Paperback: 978-1-61219-184-3
Ebook: 978-1-61219-185-0

Ⓜ MELVILLE INTERNATIONAL CRIME

Happy Birthday, Turk!
Jakob Arjouni
978-1-935554-20-2

More Beer
Jakob Arjouni
978-1-935554-43-1

One Man, One Murder
Jakob Arjouni
978-1-935554-54-7

Kismet
Jakob Arjouni
978-1-935554-23-3

Brother Kemal
Jakob Arjouni
978-1-61219-275-8

The Craigslist Murders
Brenda Cullerton
978-1-61219-019-8

Death and the Penguin
Andrey Kurkov
978-1-935554-55-4

Penguin Lost
Andrey Kurkov
978-1-935554-56-1

The Case of the General's Thumb
Andrey Kurkov
978-1-61219-060-0

Nairobi Heat
Mukoma wa Ngugi
978-1-935554-64-6

Black Star Nairobi
Mukoma wa Ngugi
978-1-61219-210-9

Cut Throat Dog
Joshua Sobol
978-1-935554-21-9

Brenner and God
Wolf Haas
978-1-61219-113-3

The Bone Man
Wolf Haas
978-1-61219-169-0

Resurrection
Wolf Haas
978-1-61219-270-3

Come, Sweet Death!
Wolf Haas
978-1-61219-339-7

Murder in Memoriam
Didier Daeninckx
978-1-61219-146-1

A Very Profitable War
Didier Daeninckx
978-1-61219-184-3

Nazis in the Metro
Didier Daeninckx
978-1-61219-296-3

He Died with His Eyes Open
Derek Raymond
978-1-935554-57-8

The Devil's Home on Leave
Derek Raymond
978-1-935554-58-5

How the Dead Live
Derek Raymond
978-1-935554-59-2

I Was Dora Suarez
Derek Raymond
978-1-935554-60-8

Dead Man Upright
Derek Raymond
978-1-61219-062-4

The Angst-Ridden Executive
Manuel Vázquez Montalbán
978-1-61219-038-9

Murder in the Central Committee
Manuel Vázquez Montalbán
978-1-61219-036-5

The Buenos Aires Quintet
Manuel Vázquez Montalbán
978-1-61219-034-1

Off Side
Manuel Vázquez Montalbán
978-1-61219-115-7

Southern Seas
Manuel Vázquez Montalbán
978-1-61219-117-1

Tattoo
Manuel Vázquez Montalbán
978-1-61219-208-6

Death in Breslau
Marek Krajewski
978-1-61219-164-5

The End of the World in Breslau
Marek Krajewski
978-1-61219-274-1

Phantoms of Breslau
Marek Krajewski
978-1-61219-272-7

The Minotaur's Head
Marek Krajewski
978-1-61219-342-7

The Accidental Pallbearer
Frank Lentricchia
978-1-61219-171-3

The Dog Killer of Utica
Frank Lentricchia
978-1-61219-337-3